MESSIAHS

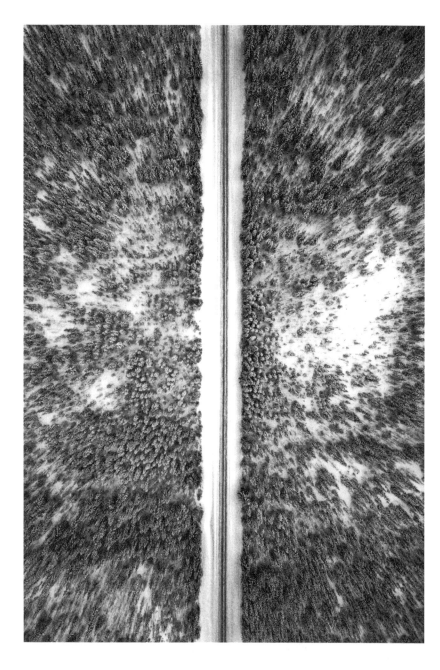

MESSIAHS

MARC ANTHONY
RICHARDSON

TUSCALOOSA

FC2 is an imprint of the University of Alabama Press

Inquiries about reproducing material from this work should be addressed
to the University of Alabama Press

Book Design: Publications Unit, Department of English, Illinois State
    University; Director: Steve Halle, Production Assistant: Lars Avis
Cover design: Lou Robinson
Cover image: art by Jr Korpa, courtesy of the artist, https://jr-korpa.com
Typeface: Adobe Caslon Pro

Library of Congress Cataloging-in-Publication Data is available from
the Library of Congress.

ISBN: 978-1-57366-190-4
E-ISBN: 978-1-57366-892-7

What is this gypsy passion for separation, this
readiness to rush off—when we've just met?
My head rests in my hands as I
realize, looking into the night

that no one turning over our letters has yet
understood how completely and how
deeply faithless we are, which is
to say: how true we are
to ourselves.

Marina Tsvetaeva

Once a man becomes a wife they are a new creature and should be addressed as such, he says to her, whispers, for women listen for whispering men, for their fathers with the force of a folktale in the black of their beds at night in the cabins of north country—a northeasterly tryst for this woman of Asian and this man of African antecedents, both birthed in this modern American state, one of the five that has embraced the proxy initiative—whispers with those coywolves crying outside now in the snow, after conjuring the couple of men on the row with him who had just severed their scrota: anathemas for the death house. No, she does not know why he's thinking about this, she thinks. Yes, she knows why he's thinking about this, she thinks: the quail eggs at supper, the white plate, the spilled wine upon them—and the astonishing effect of red on white—and then the way the scrota lay there outside the feed slots of the men's single white cells at dawn: not like shaven little skin sacs, with their testes attached to their tunicae, but like bloody little newborn rats—but before this the screaming the adrenaline and the quiet stench of iron in the air with this fortitude it took to stay standing, just long enough to sever and to shove yourself through a slot (their spermatic cords sawed through by blades extracted from daily safety razors? by miscellaneous bits of metal? by pork chop bones or the plastic handles of tooth-brushes ground down on the concrete for cutlery?)— for he saw all four rectangled two at a time in each sac all bloody and burgundy in his hand mirror after his forearm shot through the feed slot of his single white cell at dawn—the vertical bars in the square above the slot being too close together to squeeze a forearm through, akin to a cashier's window, with the more spaced-apart bars *around* the window sheeted with white metal mesh (as it was with *all* the cells and is still: white blood cells)—his acrylic shaving mirror angled downwardly and just right to reflect the reversed and inverted images onto his retinae to be righted by the brain, for first the mirror was facing the northeast then the southwest and then the northeast again with each time needing to be handled by the opposite hand, for they were on either side of him these men and he was between them—*testis* (witness), yet *testis unus, testis nullus* (for you would need another to corroborate this sight in your head, for the testimony of one is to be dis-regarded unless corroborated by the testimony of another, for there's no video surveillance in this ancient

2

execution unit, no way to catch the guards doing what they're ordered to do, only the other hand mirrors looking out on the row with you)—so then Fucking Christ! Fucking Christ! one of the guards cries, above a plash of footgear, for this guard still cries in his head as they must've lain there these two crimsoning men inside the leucocytes of their separate cells, a malady to society to either side of him, one white and one black and both outrageously stark naked, passed out from the shock or from the bloodlack, prostrate or faceup on the concrete, coolness against the red warmth rippling out and with their cocks now monstrously clitoral. But as he is saying again to her that once a man becomes a wife they are a new creature and should be addressed as such she is already in the kitchen in her mind and then later in her body because she can't stand to be in bed with him anymore, because there's this shitty kitchen in my belly, she thinks, the wine and the excuse for giving him my bed and I must need to organize this shit, she thinks, fueled by the burgundy while cutting on the lights, with hope and with scrubbing and holding my boy up high by the waist to wipe his lil' Buddha! I need to dunk my hands in water. I need to fill this fucking kitchen up with scalding hot water—this sink! I need to go outside and stoop in the snow and plunge them in hold them in and then rush them into this sink—oh God! the hum in my hands: the burn. So there is a scalding after she rushes in and she is calm and thinking of that sea again: *I need to think of the sea every now and again,* she once wrote to him, *for I am forgetting him. I am not normal. I need to feel the warm warm seawater like bathwater, for I never want to forget how warm the seawater was, like bathwater,* she wrote, to lead up to *her,* to explain *her*—for it had been over a year and a half then since she'd seen any ocean or her at all, her mother, and now over three years have passed—*nor forget the clownfishes I saw swimming inside of it deep sea diving, those small orange bodies with their bold white vertical bars accented by black, how those protandrous tropical harlequins can engender both genders and live symbiotically among the death sting of the sea anemones, how the biggest fish the queen clownfish the only female fish in a school of male fish stresses the next biggest fish, the male mate, and stresses the male and stresses the male to keep the mate male, who then stresses the remaining males, for though being born males the decrease of cortisol will turn the males into females, but when she dies—she is bound to die—the male mate will become larger and rise to the rank of the female alpha stressor, whereas the next biggest will become larger and rise to the rank of the new male mate.* But by and by as this cycle began afresh *in this supermax,* he wrote back, responding to her missive, redolent of her vaginal scent smeared across it, his spent semen smeared across his, *the hierarchy is reversed: it is the* least *of the males who are turning female in their standard prison attire, orange accented by bars painted white while living among the sting of the death house for years . . . . The administration and the warden and the guards have all stretched out those men those lovers so supremely those lovers who will never*

4

touch each other from separate cells that I, who was centered between them like a muscular pump, could feel them both thrumming their deoxygenated desires through a heart that just had to oxygenate and deliver them respectively and readily and aided and abetted them unknowingly: the dawn of that double self-castration when the light is coming through the windows and stretching knife-like down the corridor to our row to my door is when we do it, he wrote back, he must've wrote back, the black lover to the white, or at least as I imagine him, because neither of them had a watch nor wanted one and he would've romanticized the moment as only a madman would do. I aided that note those notes—for there are no clocks no cameras no way to catch the guards doing what they're ordered to do, as guards are wont to do, to keep the quiet in here—I aided those notes, as did the man before me for as you know, as you know, I have been on this row now for over a year, but they, the black lover and the white, have both been here for over a decade and the dead man before me in this cell only did it for something from the commissary, aided their correspondence for a pack of gum a candy bar a couple of cigarettes, which could be passed along as well. I did it for free. Though I could've been caught—I should've been caught—and consigned to administrative segregation, thus losing my daily hour outside inside a kennel among other things and my good standing too, for returning to solitary requires less justification than when a man first entered it, that space with no sound no soul no sunlight, only the dimmed lights of an eerie florescent twilight as you lose some eyesight and your perception of

5

depth, the phenomenology of an alien world where the nimbuses of a lover's nipples hover above you and the shit beside you and the silence is often broken by cockroaches and mice scuttling around like the sound of the shells being peeled away from your hard-boiled eggs, where every little detail is constantly eating you alive: the smell of the after-shave of a trial witness, the bags under a mother's eyes, the smirk of an arresting officer, the smell of bacon, a corner you could've turned and the bedbugs a breath being the dinner bell: the carbon dioxide exhaled in sleep and the waking up to their Lilliputian shits smeared across the sheets, each having swiped a blood payment: everlasting vigilantes that can fit into a crack the slimness of a credit card—yes, he wrote this, the man, but not for the woman, for fear of the officials, for with a few sheets already written, for this reason, he had *ended* the missive after writing *while living among the sting of the death house for years* and just signed off with his disgust, disgusted at what wasn't inveighed against and never would be, yet throughout that night, on separate sheets, he continued to write and reread and rewrite, as writers are wont to do, words he would destroy soon after he was finished with them before falling asleep, only to rewrite them again the next night and on later nights, destroying them every day (though the writing was still a terrible risk, for his cell could've been tossed at anytime), but he had needed to write them so he wrote and destroyed and rewrote them after memorizing what he would have to always undo, as *prison* writers are wont to do, kept writing from memory *the admin-*

istration and the warden and the guards have all stretched *out those men* and so on and so on and over and over these words that would never be sent, only torn up and flushed away again and again—*and so, yes, I helped them. I helped them with those notes. I did it for myself. I did it for this solitude this schism of the heart and the week before they did it, during any one of our note-passing moments, they were always less than fifteen minutes away from being caught and kept whole men these men, the black lover and the white, who will now be removed to separate supermaxes once their bodies stabilize, having gone through their hemorrhagic shocks, with that black brain suffering the bloodlack the most, yes, less than fifteen minutes away from being caught and kept whole men these half men who didn't want to become whole men again but wives to each other, who would've severed their sexes entirely had they not fainted—or at least that's what the meme is, I hear, on that whole superhighway to half-truths, the gospel of the new world wide web, the gossip of that guard perhaps, the one who first found them and shouted They cut off their balls! They cut off their balls! The nigger and the redneck! (why are the men who are in love with men always and only news when they are deviant or aberrant?)—some think they're just trying to get off the row by feigning insanity, but only the incomprehension of the nature of your crime in connection to your punishment can do this—which, for a psychiatrist, can be damn near impossible to prove. I think they just want to be whole again. For they believe they were. Yet when the white was fitted for a suit the linchpin was pulled: a guard would* sashay down this row every fifteen minutes for every fifteen minutes is the standard, the watch before the death-watch cell (the holding cell of the off-site facility serving signed warrants where the white was to be transported), but I still passed along those notes between those times sometimes, those watches (and maybe even once a packaged hoard of painkillers to prepare the other for the pain—or maybe that razor blade for the white? God knows how he got it), passed along those notes for the last week they were to be together, for no one can talk along the row and an echo can carry you away on a gurney if you want (the sounds of the standard televisions and radios inside the cells—for those who can afford them and are in fairly good standing—are suppressed by near-defunct headphones), so there are only footfalls and flushes and farts and snores and coughs and sloshes and trickles and drips, and after a guard would pass by and his footsteps had faded away one of the lovers would stick his acrylic shaving mirror through the feed slot to scan up along the row—for our arms are not only blocked by bars but by white metal mesh—and once the coast was clear he would take up a long piece of yarn wrapped around a weighted note and would wind the other end around a forefinger and whisper for me, then reach out to swing the weight over to my slot where I would snatch it and swing it to the other lover, after whispering for him, and then vice versa later (a pack of gum a candy bar a couple of cigarettes: all had passed along this way, possibly even permitted by the guards, the lax ones), but it has been a week out and—though I've been asked about it—I have yet to be connected to it, nor do I believe

I ever will be, for that guard is gone, the one who first found them, a lax one who had handed out to everyone other than the white lover that day those daily safety razors to be collected later—because maybe a few days before this the white had distracted the guard, and was not just cursing him without a care, from checking and seeing that that daily safety razor, the one the black was handing back to him, was missing its razor blade? Maybe he—not me—had helped them with those notes? For money, for money from a relative of theirs? Or maybe it was a trustee, an inmate in the warden's favor, who mopped the floors delivered the food retrieved the trays, for now one's been replaced by another. And of course they could've communicated in codes through the ventilation vents in the rear— though not so effectively—during the day when the guards would converse crassly or after they'd yell up Mail up! Chow up! Shower up! For a rower—for we are always undertaking this awful rowing toward God—is always alone in the dayroom or in a stall of the communal kennel outside for his one hour a day, six days a week. He eats alone. He sleeps alone. He fades away. But not before he would whisper. So I aided them, as did the man before me, with the bosom of a Jehovah! Jehovah! as I am called and always called by the guards here as jeer, Jehovah! Jehovah! one can call along the corridor, outside this row, and an echo can carry for a year—an echo can carry for a year. Yet now, standing over this cabin kitchen sink, drunk and cold and only hearing the cries of the coywolves outside, the woman only knows about the basics of this obliterated part of the letter, this ghostlike coda,* from what the man wrote to her; she will never read any of its lines unless they are written once again by him, from memory, only to be destroyed once more, by her, burned inside her furnace—as *all* his missives had to be—so she could remain in the now and only the now and never be undone—for she *may* need to deca-thect from him: the phone call today made her remember. The phone call. It is late December now, and the promise she may soon have to keep would require a neutrality and surely, she thought with fore-thought, back in late June, when her lover was soon to be released, letters from a once-condemned man to a now-condemned woman could be more dangerous in the forest once he's released and reads them after I leave him and—what if his mind escapes, again? The coy-wolves have been crying ever since she left the bed—those wendigos in the snow—and once they get full on the howling you cannot tell one from another or how many they really are. She remembers him mentioning the madmen, but never until now his link to them, and the perfect penmanship of his hand and his body now lying on her bed as she stands before the sink, feeling that her hands have been slightly seared by this scalding water, as *his* conscience is momentarily cleared as he sleeps like a feather unburdened by flight, the slight snore and—will he be sleeping with you tonight, or below, that face of the cause célèbre? If he were a killer, she thinks, asleep, he would be innocent. All killers are. *There is no discernible difference between killing a child and killing a sleeping man*—for what is a man other than a child who has not yet woken up? Yet *he* has, hasn't he? Yet some thought and still think, she thinks, he was a *fool* for taking the initiative, not just for a claimed killer, but for a person with so little promise. Yet since this person is—no, no, must not think of him and his tonight, but of *me* and *mine*. Though mine has never thought of me. Yet will he be sleeping with you tonight? Do you even want him to and—what is this taste in my mouth? She spits into the kitchen sink, and then looks above it into the black window mirror: another December snowstorm will be rearing its head tonight—the forecast called for it; soon the white winds will be roaring over the timber of this crazy, aging cabin, for since the man arrived here in mid-November—free for five months now—he has been working on several essays for the debut book, down below in her cabin that's not truly a cabin, for it has the depth of a house and the animus of a furnace and it sleeps and speaks like a crucible sometimes; it is lodged in a slope like an axe, a lonely two-level liminal house halved crosswise by the incline to dominate a skeletal snowy valley of larches and birches and ashes, of various evergreens—a bottomless abyss right now at night, the vale of the forest—with doors opening out back below on the bottom floor and above in the front. The woman has been sleeping with the man most of the time, sometimes in her bed and sometimes in his, for these lovers have separate rooms on separate floors and still appear to be beginning a new life sequestered together in this crystalline forest; she in her late thirties and he in his early forties, with many solitary years between them; she having begun hers even before moving here over three years ago and he before the two years and three months and three days *inside*: she in a lifeless wedlock and he with a writer's want—and should they be unneurotic for the eighty-eight more days here, a Mercurian year, the ice may begin to thaw, much too early these years, and it would be the first day of spring. The first day of spring. A ladybug alights on the faucet. The wine is waning. The phone call is fresh: that early morning message, that voice the woman hadn't heard in over three years, that voice from the old country in this country now seeking the *other* old country within her—for though the woman was neither born nor raised in it, the old country, she has been and is still being steered by it, the ways of it: the voice spoke for the way of it. So that standing over this sink, the kitchen lights so bright, she is still looking out of the black window mirror at the would-be-seen snow-covered evergreens encroaching on the would-be-seen snow-covered quarter-mile drive of dirt, those would-be-seen boughs and branches reaching toward it, as it in turn reaches toward the route: after finalizing her divorce, she had fled to the forest with only minimal stays in the university town for the winters—this being her first winter in the forest with her lover—leaving her neighbor to tend to the cabin's upkeep and to clear the drive with his snowplow; while during the other seasons she would take in boarders most of the time, Bhikkhunis, sisters between sojourns. But now that aftertaste again. Salty. So she swipes the ladybug from the faucet, draws a glass of water, drinks it, and then looking again into the black window mirror becomes afraid and thinks that there's something dark about them, that there's something grotesque about them: mirrors—as if they are really one-way mirrors concealing insidious instruments; if only they could be portals between two possibilities, gateways to a reversed world where there aren't any religious sects of morality creeping into your personality, where there aren't any proxy initiatives to mutely pressure you, where the bereaved aren't the capital killers and the capital killers aren't the bereaved: Ah, she thinks, a chiasmus to be considered inside a court. So she cuts off the lights and in the dark can see the play of the humpbacked gibbous moon on the snow and says to herself—Oh! An epiphany on a tombstone, perhaps, an epitaph?—and then all at once she is tasting the amniotic salinity of the ocean in her mouth, drowning again, like before like always before and she must think of something *anything* else to oust this ocean from her mouth, this tiny body in her brain, for the aftertaste of his semen returns it, this goddamn ocean in my mouth, and then thinks of why she hasn't sucked a cock in years until now and doesn't miss it and then of her anus opening up like a mouth before he stuffed it into my mouth then stuffed my shit into my mouth and so she walks right back into her room and plops down beside him and says You can't come in me anymore, as he starts and sits up in her bed, rubbing his eyes, the lamp the only thing. What? What? the man says, afraid—and yet is angered now: he thought he was still on the row. No longer is the woman naked as he is, for after rolling out of bed with the excuse of needing to do something in the kitchen, she had gathered up her thermals and slippers from the rug and just left, not even bothering to dress. *What? What?* But the woman is silent now, sitting on the side of her bed, looking ahead, and in the lamplight, with her back straight and her breasts scarcely defined, her frame lean and truculent, her eyelids pulled narrow at the corners by crow's-feet, the bones of her pyramidal cheeks, the square jaw and the jet-black buzz cut peppered with salt—like a Buddhist nun's—she looks quite handsome. She is focused now, yet unclear. Love, the man says, hanging his head without saying another syllable, just lumbering up to lighten the bed, leaving a warm depression, and standing nakedly over her— his ebon skin, his greying crown of kinks, his long curly eyelashes and that single eyebrow curled into a horn, his tall frame and thin girdle of fat making his midriff fatherly, his sex now hanging like a lynching— before dropping to a knee. Let me see, he says. The past is two doors down. And so she blurts out You're too vile you're too much! I'm not you I'm not normal! I should've never destroyed them, those faces—I forgot his face! How could I forget his face? It was a face only a mother must forget, only a mother must forego. I only see my father's now. The dark-skinned face of her lover is before her, his body below her, her *shadow* developed into the third dimension and she

14

thinks: Why am I so solaced by the darkest of men? For she is only now hearing what he said: Let me see—and it is uncanny, for another had said the same thing to her over three years ago, a blue-black man in a morgue. The man is sitting on his heels as he lays his head in the woman's lap. Let me see, he says, and then her palm is on the back of his neck, pressing quietly, her thermal leggings and her heat is in his face, feeling the pressure at his base—and she can break it if she wants. If she wants. But her hips rise a bit after he lifts his head away. A mother's grief, she sighs, opening her thighs, becomes the door she walks through for the rest of her life—opens them, for he has slid off her leggings and slippers and is lowering his head again, her palm pressing his nape again—she can shut it, she says, eyes shut, but there will always be the temptation to touch it, to open it—and then she snaps his neck like a tooth-pick. The dream she had many years before and forgot about until now and she smiles and thinks about how *good* it is to be no longer lost and lulled and is *relieved* by this already-dreamt marker, as if there were no lapse between them, the then and the now, as though this route is the right route thus far for the moment, and then she forgets it again and is lying again on her back, lifting her thermal undershirt to bare her small breasts, and then wetting her fingertips with her spittle: beyond the junction of her motherly thighs a blue-black basement is flooding and brimming and a bucket of water and a bucket of water and a bucket of water out a window would never be enough: a great voidance is needed, by way of a path of least resistance; so her knees spire above his head for her feet to perch on his shoulders, her feed slot to his mouth to receive the excess water, and soon she imagines a small skeleton flushing out with the rush and onto the coral reef of his oral cavity and begins to weep and moan as his tongue muscles and circles the crease between the glans and the hooded cloak, cinching the inner cape, tightening her sluice laterally, hugging it, this organ of taste turning intromittent organ, her pelvis grinding away at the precipice of her bed and his long, coarse beard, her eyes shut, rapt: a yellow eagle swoops down from a sun and seizes her, snatches her up from the river and back into the blurring orb, so that then: oblivion. Her feet alight on the rug, so he lies down beside them. Both, she and he, are still. She lying halfway on her bed, her thermal undershirt half-raised, her breasts and sex showing, and he lying naked on the rug, a three-dimensional shadow and so I had, she says, as though she's been speaking, what I believe to be the second visitation from my father: in the light he looked fantastic and wore a great suit, he was very energetic and joyful and kept saying and saying let's go for a ride let's go for a ride, let's ride the wild horses, and I remember I remember saying to him that *everything* is so rapid-fire with him, as if to say he was being pushy and overbearing and I wanted to be left alone, then he sat down in a chair like a child, with a sad tranquility to him, so I leaned over and held his face in both hands and said, very tenderly: My God— you are so full of life—I forgot you are dead . . . .

The copper washbasin cups the sunbeam in the bathroom as nothing now, the buck head branches antlers across the apricot wall in shadow as nothing now, as the son of sovereigns and slaves, stepping from the shower stall, the ebon man of exigency is nothing momentarily: in this interstice, when nothing is present, the principle is so infinitesimal that nothing *is* principle: the absolute end of knowledge. God cannot be the object of knowledge, just as a knife cannot cut itself, nor a fire be burnt. God is an enigma to God, an eternal I do not *know* what I am, nor what I am not. God is not a being but a state of being. God is love. And love cannot be the object of desire: desire is a prisoner, a prisoner who dreams that he can only see his lover in reflections (for when there is no reflection he is unable to see, and when there is no seeing he is unable to reflect), who views another prisoner's idyllic picture in his hand mirror outside his cell (for his hands are always apt to do what his body cannot), and who embellishes specific mentions from vaginally scented missives (for the feeling began with the exchanging of bodily fluids in missives: *Hold me open,* she always opens, with a lingering almond odor or a particular piscine scent always present still even after it has long since passed from carrier to sorter to be postmarked then approved by some administrative censor): he sees the pale blue veins of her thighs as exquisite and sinuous as pine needle shadows on the sunlit snow outside, he sees the faint flush in her face as darkly romantic as smoke against glass, he sees her fallow sex as she vows to keep it without him asking or even expecting it, he sees her childlike expression of joy that would be difficult to counterfeit, and he sees the lone white stroller under the streetlights of her nights, stalking her slowly from spotlight to spotlight, as this scintillant trickle of water travels now down the window in broad daylight, from one cluster of condensation to another. But no. Love cannot be the object of desire: love is the absolute end of everything. The man returns and wipes away the condensation from the bathroom mirror, towels himself and puts on his robe. He starts his sets of deep breathing, taking air into his lungs, expanding them to capacity, and then holding for several seconds before slowly exhaling; three times he does this: three, deep, breaths. Thank you, he says, to her, alone. It has been a few days since the recent snowstorm and his lover has driven the twelve miles into town to be with the Buddhist nuns, who lecture at the university, run seminars: she is the administrator of the Religious Studies division, for she is not a believer in any one religion, and neither is he. He is grateful for where he has landed, outside the city outside the cries, with only one man in this cabin for now with a forest for a father, a winter wonderland for sure, a metropolis of trees as far as the eye can see—in this last sentence of December: the month of transparency. Even this bathroom is bigger than his cell, he thinks, a cell the size of a parking space: the man before him in that cell had stood against the back wall and traced himself with a pencil and then shaded himself in so lightly that, after he first entered the cell, he didn't see it for a week, and when he *did* see it he couldn't *unsee* it and had to sleep in that dead man's bed and stare into his shade and shrink into his head for over two long years that could've been much much shorter—having forfeited the right to appeal, and without that stay, that stay of execution—with that shady figure developing into the third dimension at night in half-light sometimes to sit beside him in bed and attempt to converse with him in some sort of sinister sign language that he could never decipher, of which one sign *should've* been clear, but he couldn't know for sure if that shady hand was waving hello or goodbye, for as soon as it returned to the wall, as though it had forgotten something, it always finished with a few more flying signs; sometimes he would wonder if this recurring dream belonged to him or to the previous man, supersaturating the mattress, which was nothing more than a thin cotton cushion covering a shelflike metal frame protruding from a wall; sometimes he would want to erase the shade altogether, from mind and matter, yet he hated the thought of erasing the rich remnants of a man. It could've been worse, he thinks, inside his cabin bathroom—he has thought the thought before, many times before, as though he were writing about it, as though he is writing about it now, for his thoughts are often orderly and essayistic before he sits down to write them, that practice he honed in prison—it wasn't as bad as it could've been: those white walls of bars with their white metal mesh, made all the more deplorable by the grime, were much better than those newer execution cells across the state—which are similar to the cells in that solitary unit, administrative segregation—small, seedy cinder block rooms with solid steel doors fixed with shatterproof window slits and feed slots locked from the outside, or filthy metal contraptions, like gas station deal drawers—so that passing a note or a pack of gum or a candy bar or a couple of cigarettes would be perfectly impossible—so I was fortunate, he thinks, and I wasn't inside for so long as most, though I still lost my mind, for what I was *in* there for was so supremely absurd that it made all the *other* absurdities seem quite sensible to me and that stay could've been taken away at any time—so my mind is *still* fucked up and my bowels are backed up and my shit is really killing me! And now his heart depresses his chest, for his robe is off and he is sitting over the commode. God thank God, he thinks: his stool is stable still, a good reading, an ouroboros in a bowl—for it wasn't always like this before: there were the occasional periods of constipation for over two months, up until last week, perhaps brought on by the change of medication; but before this, five months ago, immediately after his release, for a few days he had suffered the antithesis, a frequent flow of diarrhea, for he was *liquefying* inside that cell before his release and that adulterated blast-chilled prison food—the same served in city schools— would also have him vomiting like an African god, creating a galaxy inside the commode; so he was lonely and sick, watching a lonely and sick world swirling away beneath him. Many men and women exonerated from capital cases suffer the same symptoms as veterans of war: post-traumatic stress, schizophrenia, severe depression, suicidal tendencies, and constant constipation from all the medications: the ad hominem attacks of death row syndrome. Only now—eleven years since the initiative's inception—is there a conversation about what a proxy must endure—after an exoneration: for there has never been one before. A proxy, as the man was known officially, is more similar to the war veteran than the common death row inmate of the past thirty years could ever be—because they were *both* volunteers, as was the proxy's executioner: the state, a debtor, would pay one volunteer after the other pays the debt for the debtor to the state. But if an executioner wants to forfeit his duty, indeed, he may do so. But the proxy, even if he wishes to renege, is still committed to the injection chamber and the worst thing to have to feel, he thinks, back in his robe, is the irreversible sting of your mercy. Goddamn. I drove to that court. I surrendered to it. After kissing my sister goodbye, by taking her son's place in handcuffs and leg-irons with a tether chain, for it must've been a calculated cruelty, he thinks, writing in his head for that future account, my God, the world one must see along the way on the way there could cause anyone to renege—for this would be the next to the last chance to do it—and consequently the condemned—like a dog waiting to die in a kennel—whether falsely convicted or not, is forced to cook in a county jail with twisted mixed feelings and to sulk and see if their sacred family member would come and suffer for them or not; and even if the condemned is opposed to a proxy—out of guilt or grief or love—he has *no* right to refuse a proxy and so and so this quandary could create another kind of cruelty: the murder of oneself, now or later. Or perhaps he might eventually reform—which is the initiative's intent, this system of state-sanctioned sacrifice—through contrition and mortification, through our Lord Jesus Christ, that sect ought to say, that right-left religious sect, adherents to the initiative—washed in the blood of a lamb by way of a Paschal Pardon, a Blood Law: misnomers for the initiative, appropriated for political propaganda (the former based on an ancient Judaic law, freeing capital prisoners at Passover, and the latter on an indigenous belief that the souls of the slain require reprisal for peace). Only a first-degree murderer convicted of *one* count of murder of an *adult* from a different family is open to the initiative—even if an aggravating factor is rape—and the family of the victim must approve the proxy option, for they are always of the faith, though they don't have to be, nor does the family of the offender; but almost all of the proxy-freed offenders, as they are known, and many of their family members, have fervently converted, for the executions are always attended by audiences and avid reporters, for the initiative conceals and has concealed from its conception an obsession *obliged* by mass communication: an unhealthy preoccupation with a rite of sacrifice as dark as the River Styx. The executioner, he thinks, in his robe, may have many weeks to decide whether or not to execute a sentence, and can refuse to do so even at the point of execution—though subjecting himself to legal penalties—yet I had only one week after my nephew's sentencing hearing to decide whether I would die for him or not—and I could never renege: after swearing before the court, after signing the documents, for all intents and purposes his capital case would become mine, his timeless time would become mine—for the condemned are always suspended between two times: conviction and execution—any process toward clemency would be undertaken for me in the form of a pardon, and *I* would have to sign the appeal waiver, not my nephew—*every* proxy has to sign an appeal waiver—but still, for all intents and purposes my nephew's court-appointed attorney would have to prove *my* innocence, as I waited to get lucky or to be killed by people who wanted nothing from me, who were not angry with me, but who were authorized to kill me in a tranquil manner free of moral and legal liability—for unless the sentence was reversed or preceded by my natural death suicide or murder, it would have to be executed by that *other* volunteer: and then a debtor would pay him after *I* had paid the debt for *this* debtor. A chiasmus that would kill you every day, that would seep into your subconscious like a crime. Your nephew would become a virus. No matter how much you love him, before you're executed, you would come to loath him. No matter how innocent or deficient he is, believing him at fault, you would come to betray him—and then you would die and die and die! But *all* death row inmates die a slow and painful psychological death before the state ever executes them. Many will be broken beyond repair, after years and years of waiting—decades—their minds gone before their bodies are and their *lives* already forgotten, a Sisyphean warfare in which death is a fait accompli, a formality already accomplished in spirit, as the state concludes its premeditated murder by putting the dead to death a second time—or the dead might do it themselves: Time for seconds, they say, before hanging up. *Suicides have a special language,* he once wrote to her, his lover. *Like carpenters, they want to know which tools.*

They never ask why build. But you want to know about the unit. You want to know about where we live: this ancient execution unit is the two sides of a cell block, three rows or tiers; each side of a row has twenty-one cells, the first cell being a shower cell, so that the unit can hold as many as one hundred and twenty condemned men—a capacity which has already been filled, so we will be spilling into another block soon; there is a cage that is only accessible from a corridor at the start of each row, from which three guards can control all one-hundred-and-twenty-six sliding doors, including those of the shower cells, as well as the doors from the corridors to the rows and everyone is quiet and at midnight the ceiling lights are the only thing left on: row three never gets completely dark, row two is dark in the back and light in the front, and row one sleeps the best—though row two and three can read and write throughout the night. I am on row two and half asleep and half awake. A liminal being. Last week I had a dream that the unit was filling up with water, that there was a great flood and we were all still locked in our cells and waiting to be drowned, for all the guards had evacuated the unit except for this one who was still running around and trying to free all one hundred and twenty of us with his one key, for the keys to the control cages had been taken, and while the water rose over the heads of the men on row one who were all asleep and couldn't be saved who couldn't be saved he ran up to row two and turned into a cockroach, and then half the men were trying to step on him while the rest remained asleep, and as the water rose higher and higher I could hear the cries of the men on row three, who were all awake, and could see the cockroach swimming in the water over my head. And in that moment, that breath, I was flooded with so much affection for it, so much love, that I saw how precious all life is. And I wanted the cockroach to make it. I wanted the cockroach to make it. The man shuts off the faucet. The sunbeam is broken: unillumined water. In his bathroom, in his robe, his attention is fixed on the steaming water in the stoppered copper basin, but now he is razoring the perimeters of his beard, trimming it, clouding the water with shaving cream; he submerges his face in the water, reemerges to towel it, and witnesses a ladybug alighting on the faucet: there is an infestation of these half-spheres here, hibernating in the house, overwintering wherever there's a hint of humidity, as if a divine power were presiding over this place—for a numen summoned them here, the lovers, away from their respective corners in this state, for this crazy, aging cabin has such a powerful personality that it educes obedience. A numen presided over that supermax as well, in the country far west of here, a private for-profit prison that is too new to be old and too old to be new, for that ancient execution unit was once a general population unit until massive additions were constructed in the epoch of the narcotics war by the right-left front to accommodate the mass incarceration rate, so that this supermax—one of many—provides a steadily flowing revenue for one of the foremost correction corporations in the country; that ancient execution unit saw the old ways and the worst; the old ways when the rowers—for the man calls them rowers—could congregate in the dayroom or outside in the communal kennel that was wide open and nine feet high, so that they could play a low-ceilinged game of volleyball, even in the snow, with that chain-link ceiling graciously scraping their knuckles; the worst was when the kennel was used for fights, for gladiatoring, the guards arming two rival rowers for a face-off—usually a black and a white or a black and a brown—with pork chop bones ground down on the concrete for cutlery, where a rower was allowed to murder or maim or rape another rower and to carve *good pussy* into a buttock; but now a rower is always isolated in a divided dayroom or in the communal kennel outside, partitioned by walls and beams and painted cement, installed in a filthy little locked stall with an *eight*-foot-high ceiling-fence, or alone in the library adjacent to the two; when the unit was designated the execution unit, on both sides of the cell block, the warden had all six thousand, two hundred and twenty-two panes of clear glass—facing out onto the variable clouds in the sky—replaced by frosted panes, so that now a rower would never find himself surprised at how *meticulously* he would preoccupy himself with anything readily available, when there are no real moments worth remembering, for he has day and he has night, he has day and he has night: he would make beautiful artificial dentures from a plastic cigarette package if he had to, for maybe the four front teeth of one of his two mad neighbors are missing, and his upper lip keeps falling in when he sleeps, when he snores; of course visits would be the highlights, especially if they're from the media, a way to get the word out, but if he has to undergo an arbitrary body cavity strip search for every non-contact visit—Open your mouth, stick out your tongue, show me your hands, turn them over, pull your foreskin back, lift up your sac, turn around, show me your soles, bend over and spread your buttocks—if he has to undergo this for a few straight days, let alone a week, he would become somewhat mortified whenever the media arrives; but when the media visits taper off, when he is no longer as relevant to the moment, when he is rarely noted on a loved one's monthly calendar—for the long drives from the city along the state's rural roads would become too strenuous and too time-consuming to make between work weeks—he will essentially become a nonentity: for who are we but our relations and our relationships? About a year after he had entered that ancient execution unit, a woman wrote to his sister, an Asian woman from in-state, from north country—about a half a year after her *own* brother had been condemned, though not as a proxy—and soon after writing his sister this woman wrote to him. She had heard of him through a film that featured him and others like him as part of a publicity campaign, which was *possibly* keeping him alive because of the public outcry, for a stay of execution had been given. Both of their families, his and the Asian woman's, had been given proxy approval—for approval must be given by the family of the victim—and proxy cases are rare—which is why the media covers them so extensively—commonly occurring in counties reflecting a dense majority of those who voted for the initiative, a right-left proposition introduced by a media mogul-politician. This Asian woman's family may have been permitted the proxy option—having her explicitly in mind—yet she just didn't feel any allegiance toward them, because they'd disowned her over a year and a half before, and still do, a year and a half later—for more than three years now. The woman's brother was sent to another supermax and installed in one of those new cinder block cells with its solid steel door and its sliding metal box—for though he is of the affluent, the fortunate, he is *un*fortunate: the *unofficial* aggravating factor of his offense would not allow for anything other than the harshest accommodations; his family's affluence could only procure the proxy option—for though the family of the victim are for holy reform, as a not-as-rich family, they have the upper hand. Only an immediate adult family member, as defined by law, can be given the *distinction* of taking the initiative: a spouse, a sibling, a parent, a grandparent, a child, a grandchild, a step-grandchild, a parent-in-law, a sibling-in-law, a child-in-law, an adopted family member; the woman's mother, the queen clownfish—for her animus is very strong—was understandably denied: since the victim wasn't old or disabled or sick, as decided by the family of the victim, the old or the disabled or the sick cannot be considered suitable as a substitute; there would be no equivalence, and the scale would be askew; the offender's spouse has two juvenile daughters to tend to, and the only other adult family member who is a close equivalent to the victim failed to make herself available, a week after the sentencing hearing, despite a phone call from her family's attorney— for her mother couldn't call her herself: the woman imagined her mother making her absence about something else *other* than the disownment, imagined her saying in silence that my daughter who used to be my daughter does not want to submit to the genius of her brother, who has two daughters and a wife who can still produce a son, and *keep* him, unlike my daughter, who used to be my daughter—who's not *fit* to have another one. No, her mother might say in silence, she let go of her son. I won't let go of mine. So that shame and desolation and a mounting veneration for another's altruistic vow were the reasons why the woman wrote to the man, the proxy, but after two months of writing to him in prison, her veneration would turn into anger over the phone whenever she thought of her mother and brother, and then her anger would turn into shame and fester into mortification whenever she thought of her son—who had resembled her brother in the face—so, in truth, the man thinks, sitting in his robe on the lid of his commode, she *hasn't* forgotten her son's face—for she hasn't forgotten her brother's: he only means much less to her. He had often thought about it in his cell though, of the possibility of her becoming a proxy, for only after a sentencing or a resentencing hearing can a proxy come forth—no other time—so, he thought, if the superior state court hears the appeal the attorneys are pursuing on her brother's behalf, earning a resentencing hearing based on some legal errors in the trial, if, instead of life, he were to receive another capital sentence—for the verdict would still stand—one week after the resentencing hearing, indeed, she would have another opportunity to prove her loyalty to the family—never mind the holy reform; in his cell, in the shadow of a doubt, he would wonder if she was writing to him to learn what it was like for him, in order to learn what it *could* be like for herself, but after she'd spoken to him over the phone about it, about his concern, he was wretchedly relieved, and would later recall the red words of her adamant reserve: I would *never* sacrifice myself for someone who has never even loved me, who almost ruined me, who had never even seen nor spoke nor wrote to me after the tragedy—besides, she said, the fight for *your* life is much more important to me, as well as the fight for a life with you afterward. I deserve you, she said. You belong to me. You belong to me. The man leaves his bathroom to clothe himself in the guest room, his room adjacent to the rec room, and is now moving from his room through the small hall and into the furnace room, where only red embers are burning, glowing red winks inside the black-grey ash, so he throws a newspaper page onto them and several pine cones as well, which leave sap on his fingers, lays two split logs of larch wood lengthwise, in parallel and on either side of the newspaper and pine cones, and then lays another one over them; he lights the paper with a lighter, adds some small sticks, and once the kindling catches fire he turns on the internal electric fan and soon sees the pine cones sparkle and pop, releasing a lively scent, the air oxygenating the fire, and then he closes the black metal door. He moves into the rec room and sits down at his desk and starts jotting down all his thoughts from the beginning: *Even this bathroom is bigger than my cell,* he writes, *a cell the size of a parking space,* and so on and so on and soon, once he's added more wood to the fire, the flames will be so strong and steady that they will heat every room, the eight red chambers of a double heart. For this cabin is not truly a cabin, being composed of four rooms on each floor; the top floor is her heart: the kitchen, the living-dining room, the bedroom and bath; and the bottom is his: the furnace room, the rec room, the guest room and bath. Mostly they couple and sleep in each other's beds, but sometimes they sleep alone in their own, like two separate pillars of a temple, standing together yet standing apart, sleeping directly above or below one another, while hearing the other's dreams or wanderings or water—and there can never be any wounds. For before bed, they are to be sealed with a kiss, by the wounded: After dark, my love. For the wounder to say: After dark, my sweet . . . .

On the day of deliverance, this summer past, the woman who had aided with her selfless assistance the man and his defense during the last year of his imprisonment, whose own home would soon subsume him, had deliriously received him with his sister in the lobby of the state prison—and the first touch the first kiss they shared held a vim and vigor unrivaled, their closeness no longer interrupted by the shatterproof glass of a visiting booth, through whose small circular vent only a warm breath could trace a face—and then they walked him outside with his one cardboard box of belongings, his sister and her, to welcome him back into a world of greater stimulation with a few family and friends waiting for him, having driven many miles from their cities on interstates and rural back roads, the paparazzi now dazzling him with flashing cameras and pushy questions, for proxy cases are rare—especially *male* proxies—even more those re-

33

sulting in a reversal: his is the first and only case in the five states—of the thirty death penalty states, of the fifty states—that had adopted the initiative; this summer past, the July sky was simply astonishing: it had been a turbulent year for him alone with the death of his nephew in mid-January and his subsequent lunacy—while suffering a shingles attack—and now leaning on his sister and his lover was all he could do to keep from falling apart in the presence of the paparazzi; but later, leaving a second-floor restaurant serving an East Asian cuisine, after gagging on a metal salad fork that was embarrassingly replaced by a plastic spork—for he hadn't eaten with a metal utensil in over two years—after gorging on barbecue from a brazier at the center of the table with the ambrosial smell of grilled pork marinated in red chili paste and charcoal smoke on his sleeves, he took a short fall down the stairs (for restraints are routine for a rower, during out-of-cell movement, even on his way to the shower cell his hands are cuffed behind his back; while for walks to the dayroom or the library or the communal kennel outside, for calls or visits, leg-irons with a tether chain are added, with the chain and the handcuffs attached to the front of a waist belt, so that stairs can only be taken with small, restricted steps): My God, the man wept, lying on the pavement, they reduced me to a child . . . . The woman stayed with him in a hotel, but then they stayed in other hotels, even homes, until most of the media obligations were fulfilled, compliments of the studios and the supporters across the country—for he is still the face of a controversial issue; his lover had accompanied him to the interviews and to the talk shows at first—whose sets would soon sicken him—but then his only sibling, his older sister, or his closest male friend had to take over because his lover had to leave, for he couldn't be left alone (they are all still shedding a greater light on not only the case, on the travesty of the arrest, on the ensuing tragedy, but on the death penalty itself; yet even after the nephew's innocence had come to light, since the appeal waiver had been signed, since the uncle had conceded the boy's guilt, recompense was no longer a possibility, suing the state would be impossible). During the last leg of his tour, he was to stay with his sister in their birth city before rendezvousing with his lover in her upstate town, in north country, where she had resumed her administrative duties in the Religious Studies division of her university; he stayed in his sister's apartment for nearly two months, neither writing nor reading, just watching television until, less than four months after his release, after the pain of his nephew's room, after the boy's alcohol-induced self-abusive hand-writing on the ceiling—which neither he, the uncle, nor his sister could bring themselves to cover with fresh paint—took on the form of those hand signs from the shade of his cell wall, having monetary donations in his new bank account and believing he could finish the tour, he rose and stole into a hotel, that first hotel after the fall, where after breaking away from the welcoming group of family and friends the lovers would hardly leave their room except to shop and to walk across the parking lot, where he would always avoid traversing the vacant parking spaces as though they were the white outlines of those white blood cells imprinted upon the tarmac in spite of the feeling that they felt weeks away instead of days, as though his mind had already been rushing away from them, as though everything in this vast world was rushing back to him in all of its grandness and technological glory, like those planes plying the skies and carrying away those magazine images of him to their respective coordinates across the globe, but which wouldn't change the fact that his lover had to accompany him everywhere, everyplace, because of his debilitating fear of large spaces, of being beaten, severely—which was why they would walk the parking lot: to help him to dispel it. Even the first time they made love was very difficult—her mind couldn't stop moving and his testicles were too sensitive to be touched—so they had just lain there like two dry teenagers, beached on a nuptial bed; but a while later, when they were intrepid enough to try again, she had to ease into the coitus like a cold icy ocean, forcing herself to stay in the current, until the body could be carried away—yet never to arrive anywhere; afterward, in the bath, she saw that she was bleeding, the start of her menses; he knocked on the door, was given permission to enter, and sat down beside the tub: she was rear up, propped up on her elbows, breathing heavily after holding her breath underwater; I can hold my breath for four minutes, she said, almost like a child; I just keep thinking and thinking that I'm not going to drown that I'm not going to drown—and then he leaned in and kissed her on the lips. She grinned. He kissed her again, slowly this time, and then leaned back, scanning the landscape of her body to that lagoon at the small of her back, then over the isles of her buttocks, easing a hand into that small pocket of water between them, probing with a digit, and then making a mark across a buttock in blood. Indeed, he had become so intrepid that, on their last night in this first hotel, he rose and stole down the hall with his small, restricted steps to take the stairs by himself, to walk through the lobby by himself, to stand in the middle of the parking lot in a vacant parking space by himself in full wingspan wearing a grin and a tank top and a new pair of pajama bottoms tucked away into his socks, and he was still standing there alone in the early misty morning gloom when his lover came out all hastily dressed and saw him on the tarmac and ran to hug him real tight, and then leaned back to look at him, tears in her eyes: You look like a hotdog without a bun . . . . She paired up with him for the first part of the tour, for it was very hard for him: Forgive me, he would say, on camera or on radio, I am so grateful to have this opportunity to talk with you all, you cannot imagine, but the worst thing about these talks is to *constantly* have to talk about the worst thing that has ever happened to me. Yet he knew that their interest in him as the face of a controversial issue wouldn't last for long, and that his nephew needed to be heard, so he saw the tour through, most of it. Besides, he would say, my love is making this more than manageable; she guided me and still guides me through the dark. No, she would say, in response to this, or to compliments from the hosts referencing her guidance, we had to guide and still guide *each other* through the dark (though she would never say what her dark was and still is). Yet in response to questions from the audience referencing her brother, should his appeal be heard, should he be given a *new* capital sentence (for only after a sentencing or a resentencing hearing can a proxy come forth), to these offenses, she would so *fervidly* reconfirm her fidelity to him, her lover, that by the time their tour together came to an end, as before, he would be very leery of her. For she is still the scion of an affluent family on her mother's side, a sort of employee of her parents, of two former foreigners from eastern Asia, who had risen in commerce in the old country and had come to this country and established a small empire in computer operating systems after only one generation; and though, for more than three years now, her mother considers her to be a member of the lower pecking order, an abomination, she now looks to her again to make amends. Out of an undying fidelity to her mor-ganatic husband—who died a year or so before the daughter's tragedy, a once brilliant yet anxious man born of modest stock, a chain-smoking man, for the queen clownfish had stressed the male and stressed the male to keep the mate male—she had given the daughter a small sum as scant severance: When a parent dies, she last said to her daughter, at her grandson's funeral, the past is gone. But when a child dies, the future is. So after she left her lover to the rest of his tour, in the silences of her cabin, she would still hear that same damn question being asked, over and over: Would you guide your brother as well, out of the dark? She would think of that night when she was seven or six, when after the long drive from the grandparents' country house her mother had told her father to carry her sleeping older brother from the car and into the house as she, the youngest—who was convincingly pretending to be asleep—was left inside the car and then later, listening to them in secret, she heard her mother tell her father, after he asked about their daughter's whereabouts, that she had already come in by herself and gone right to bed without a word; she would think of the photograph of her father and his mistress and daughter hidden in the molding of her mother's closet—for her mother had showed it to her when she was ten, a photograph taken unbeknownst to them, in public—and she would wonder if a woman who hides and forgets about the photograph of her husband's mistress and daughter in the molding of a closet would always wonder if it was still there, faded and degraded, after they long moved away. Yet once her lover arrived, at that small university depot, she was delirious again. He was delirious as well, slightly, and in a different way: after leaving his sister's apartment, after canceling the last leg of his tour, in that first hotel again, he drank and drank for a week.

She was working at the university, so she couldn't come down to get him in her car, nor could he rent one, for his license had expired and he was still so very uneasy—now especially—so he decided to take the buses: all three. A flight would've been faster, but his nerves would've never held up in a place as lustrous and peopled as an airport—he would've committed faux pas all over the place—and he would've *still* had to take a bus to get to her; people were too petty in the city, and all the novel technology had become so vaguely exciting that it soon became petty too, so he drank and drank in that first hotel and had only just stopped before taking this trip and was now suffering through one of his old and horrid withdrawals, the first since before his confinement and a film a sad film would keep replaying in his repentant mind after the trip: another sober self would be standing over and looking down at that shivering self rocking back-and-forth unconsciously in his seat on that second regional bus, looking like a petulant drunk, his fingers fidgeting viciously, or like a mentally retarded boy in a big black man's foreboding body (for when he was a boy, when he was alone, he used to pretend that he was retarded, whenever he needed to feel a certain quantum of compassion for himself, though this would only be realized much much later in life, in prison, during a shingles attack), his sober self would be standing over his shivering self in the dark and in the aisle of that second regional bus while everyone else was asleep, feeling so sorry for himself that his tears would flood his vision, for his sober self would be that older boy who had long stopped pretending to be retarded, and who was now saying to this shivering self, this man, If you cannot forgive him—in reference to the third self, the one who is still in prison, waiting to be snapped back like a rubber band—then we are *all* lost, for on that *first* regional bus, desperate for some solid sleep—he had been merely drifting in and out of it before then—he had taken his sister's sedative and was now wide awake and feeling feebly delirious, shaking and shivering, for an inferno of sugar was decalibrating his brain, a chemical storm tipping the balance, and even the galloping guilt of having cursed-out close friends couldn't distract him with compunction, remorse, for that would've required a certain degree of self-awareness, for even when he was on the *third* bus he was still too damn *primitive* to be abashed, for the regional buses had all been moving so slowly and deliberately that the whole goddamn trip was like some long dreary journey, going back in time and getting eerier and eerier, as he became more and more unraveled, slipping in and out of sleep, until he was now seeing the black Amish coats and cloaks mounting and peopling the bus with their old rustic fashion, one by one, surrounding him like a séance this fresh day for the rides had taken him an entire day—one way with two waits between three separate buses, from morning to morning—as those rides must've taken the enswathed-in-black bodies of the scarfed or hatted or bonneted faces of the Amish wherever they had gotten to and were now returning in those horse-drawn carriages he was seeing outside, slogging along the shoulder of the road on that cold November morning, as he was counting more cows or crows than Caucasians, for the long length of the rides had lessened the assault of the withdrawal symptoms just enough for him to count and then the counting itself, the concentration, had lessened it even more, and as he came closer and closer to his destination each provincial bus stop grew more and more indistinguishable than the last, so indistinguishable that he had had to stumble toward the driver twice to ask if he had missed his stop before pleasantly being surprised, though slightly delirious still, as the bus pulled into the small university depot: he saw his lover there, standing outside . . . .

He will be returning soon, she thinks, home from the university, she thinks. It is closed for the holiday season, yet the Bhikkhunis, the Buddhist nuns, are helping her lover with his mind, to calm it, before they go on their brief sojourn. It is January, the first week of the new year, and she is improvising a supper: this is the season for soups, for stews, for leftovers given a second life, a second chance to entice the palate with an ambrosial whiff rising now in the form of praise and steam from a light mullet stew, the fish skinned and filleted and flavored with onions and scallions and bay leaves for a soft delectable taste, for an esthesis free from the thick afterthought of meat—that final fright of the flesh—coupled with diced yellow potatoes and topped by pinches of sea salt and saffron strands, by dashes of red pepper; under the promise of shadows that have collected in the upper corners of the living-dining room and slid and spread across the ceiling and down the walls are the candles' glow on the dark oaken table, glimmering on black lacquered plates and bowls, picked up by pale buttered breads: these lambencies floating in the dusk alive; the woodstove is glowing, crackling, its fan whirring, and there is an old record player in a corner that hardly ever plays, for the natural sounds and silences are more than enough here and are rarely broken either by the radio—the television doesn't exist—yet still the old records inside their dusty cardboard sleeves are always waiting to be asked to dance by that old grey needle that is ever looking sharp: a ghostly jazz voice is chosen, an uncanny contralto, owing to the genetic genius of an extraordinary disorder that prevented the singer from reaching a classic puberty, from reaching corporeal maturity, leaving him childlike and childless with his voice androgynously high—*Thisss laaannnd iiiiiisss mmmiiin-nnnne*—and now a song is being sung once more for those self-castrated lovers from the row, *for a greatly ensouled singer serenaded them yesterday,* she once read, from one of her lover's letters, a section that was burned into a memory cell long before her furnace, *he serenaded them in absentia, with the acoustics of this unit spreading the song ubiquitously, for when the supervisor of this savagely quiet unit—where loud men are rapidly bludgeoned into dust, where even the lunatics are not allowed to be loud—came rushing in and saw his own guards enamored in the Church of the Imaginer, wooed and wounded by woe, he shouted and cursed and demanded that the culprit reveal his whereabouts, at which time a five-foot-high fragile black man of very fair skin stood up on the top tier and inserted himself—so the guards say— answering him directly—before the guards could—yet in such a respectful refined feminine voice that the supervisor fell silent, looked at his watch, shouted he had five minutes, and then stormed off the unit. Exodus came back in mid-lyric.* Ladybugs in a burner: the part of the stove that emits the gas that shapes the flame, the two charred half-spheres whole; she feels the hands of her lover slide around her waist from behind, his cheek resting upon her new growth of hair, and fleetingly feels like an hourglass again, waiting to be turned upside down; so enraptured was she in the Church of the Imaginer that she heard him come in but couldn't move, heard him pull up in the snow, for his license has been renewed and he's much more confident now, despite the occasional anxiety and the drive and the route and the tires being coated in snow; in this interstice between the musical tracks, he speaks to her susurrantly. She considers his carnal request. But now the subsequent song has begun. He feels her hips swaying, his hands following, then she turns and presses herself against him without interrupting the rhythm, arms around him: The heart can bear it all, she says. It is the first time they are dancing together; it is the first time they have danced in years, yet, when the ice begins to thaw—much too early these years— before the crystals can disappear, the first day of spring could just be the harbinger of a different kind of frost:

on the day he remembered the madmen, before he confessed that night, she had received a phone call that morning; it was a number she no longer knew, a voice she no longer needed; it came across an ocean of time over three years wide; even in this country the voice came from the old country seeking the *other* old country within her, for though she was neither born nor raised in it, the old country, she has been and is still being steered by it, the ways of it: the voice spoke for the way of it. The voice of a shibboleth and of a service done for her, a service that had gone beyond the call of any duty, so that now the speaker of the voice was expecting the same—for in her mother tongue the voice came as a sort of belated *direct* response to her long-unanswered letter, not a missive but a very short letter addressed to the speaker of the voice, who instead of writing back had just *acted* on the request in the letter, their only contact in over two years sent express mail as her lover was fading away inside a psychiatric cell. Over two weeks ago now, over the cabin's landline, the *essence* of that voice no longer needed to say what had been said before in silence—or by an attorney—no identification was needed, no salutation, no context: for the daughter knew why the mother was calling. The daughter had *always* known why the mother would call, before the letter, before the lover, she'd known since the sentencing hearing, yet the *attorney* had called instead—because the mother couldn't; she just couldn't call a disowned daughter to ask for something so ruinously outrageous and merciless as what this attorney had called her about, or she couldn't call simply out of a cast-iron intransigence, not affection or shame or fear, out of some pigheaded habit that would forever bar the rescission of having disowned the daughter, some causeless stubbornness that could even over-power any affection or shame or fear she would have for her son and yet now, after such a long legal limbo, after the fortune she had spent and was still spending on attorneys for over two years, the mother—with the assurance of the daughter's letter—had now finally relented by calling the daughter *herself*, in order to retain the last auxiliary she needed before the final battle—for yes, according to the call, there would be a resentencing hearing in March, the first day of spring, due to those legal errors in the trial. The verdict still stands, but the sentence has been vacated, for the trial was bifurcated: the first half was to decide whether the defendant was guilty or not, and the second half was to decide what now needs to be decided once more, whether the crime warrants a capital sentence or life. So now the mother may need her reserve, since she has long fulfilled the daughter's request—though neither the letter nor the request were ever mentioned by the mother or the daughter during the call—for though the daughter still isn't the daughter—as far as the mother is concerned—she very well *could be* again. Yet over two weeks ago, the mother still held onto just enough of that cast-iron intransigence—in case the daughter had or would have any inclination to renege—to not only deliver her message as a customary reminder of debt—without explicitly saying so—but as the product of an archaic custom in a stony tone of voice—for now deep inside the daughter's head, unconscious of it, the mother's voice is still running ceaselessly alongside everything else, for even now, beneath the pleasantries she is sharing with her lover over supper, over a light mullet stew, she still hears the feedback over the phone and the mental undertones nestled in the mother's words, that *essence*, that same unequivocal unsaid subtext stuffing them, that same you let my grandson pass away and you will *not* let my son do the same (same), the daughter subconsciously hearing a fraction of the feedback of what was said alongside a fraction of the feedback of what was not, as though the mental interplay, the eavesdropping, the subconscious thought-tapping of the mother by the daughter, is still creating a deepening psychic distortion—for there is an even *deeper* layer to this unsaid substrate: Neither will you do the same for the unsown son of his fertile wife (wife); only to cut to the deepest: I will destroy you if you do (do), in some form (form). The daughter told the mother that she would not attend the resentencing hearing. We didn't need you at the first (first), the mother said—in actual utterances, in actual words—but if this family is cursed (cursed), if this one goes awry (awry)—just make yourself available this time (time). And for a while there was an egregious species of silence that rarely *exists* between mother and child, a species so void of love that it could only be occupied by a black epoch of pus. Time for seconds (seconds), the daughter said, before hanging up. This was over two weeks ago. Abscesses are now her heart. Filled with pus instead of prayers. For that morning, before her lover returned from town, overwhelmed by the multiple viewpoints of culpability, she filled her bathroom sink with water with scalding water and went outside and held her hands in the snow before rushing back in to set them into the sink—and would do this once more that very night, drunk, with her lover in her bed and with those coywolves crying in the snow (something she hadn't done since her first winter after the tragedy)—staying like this for a few seconds, until she couldn't take it anymore and took them out. Then, after a while, she wiped the mirror to scrutinize the eyes that had been banished behind the mist: The masquerade is over, she said, time to put your mask back on. *If this one goes awry*, she echoed, if the sentence is the same, her mother meant—for the gravity of that unofficial aggravating factor could still prevent the commutation, which is why a rich man is on death row in the first place: an Asian man had mangled and murdered a white woman, a prominent blonde, his mistress and the mother of his bastard. But even *if* the sentence is life—in spite of the grisliness of the killing and the color and the class of the victim—her brother would have to serve it *himself*—for proxies cannot serve life, only the god of death, which is believed to be the surest way to holy reform for the proxy-freed offender. Even if he is *given* life he would still be unable to *give* life, to sow seed for a son, for conjugal visits are forbidden; he would only be able to continue to do what he does now: offer minimal assistance to the family empire from behind bars—so that his technological genius would largely go to waste. The chief reason why the family of the victim—a not-as-rich family who now has the upper hand—had permitted the proxy option at the sentencing hearing—the secondary reason being their belief in holy reform—was that a proviso of money or a small silent share of the empire had been presented to them, for these negotiations would have been clandestinely conducted; but since one of the two preapproved proxies—the other being the offender's wife, the mother of his two daughters—failed to make herself available—she never said she would or would not—since the mother in a last-minute effort to secure the deal couldn't take the initiative herself, being much older than the victim, the bargain was null. Now the mother can tell the family of the victim that the daughter will take the initiative for sure, and they'll re-allow it, for the proxy option will need to be. Yes, as outrageous and surreal as this sounds, only a *new* capital sentence can set her son free, once her daughter—who will again *be* her daughter—takes the initiative, as she promised to in the letter. Yes, the daughter has always known why the mother would call; it just took that letter for her mother to be able to call her herself, it just took that letter for her to burn her *lover's* letters, for her to throw them into the furnace—for her to remain in the now and only the now and never be undone. Over the phone, nothing really needed to be said about that letter, that very short letter, that was never even answered by a letter, for only *proof* that it had been read, only an *act* was necessary—so now only the word of the writer would need to be proven, if necessary, *if this one goes awry.* But how but how, my love, the daughter now says, sitting alone in her cabin kitchen, drinking and speaking susurrantly, not to herself but to her lover—as she *used to* speak to him in absentia—who is now sleeping in her bed, snoring slightly, having had his fill of supper and sex, how could a woman *request* this from her child, even if it's to save her other child—*especially* if it's to save her other child? How could she choose? But I guess *I* of all people should know. Maybe I was just hoping that she would release me from this debt, that she would release *herself* from collecting it? If only I were a believer it would be easier. Regardless, at least for other families, this is what the initiative has done: it persuaded and allowed the families of the offenders to choose them over another family member by coercing or allowing that other family member to do what they normally would've never done, for the sake of some sacred belief, for the sake of some hoped-for reform, of clearing the family's name; with a romanticized martyrdom in mind, with a promise of a prize in the after-here, or with a great prod of shame—despite not being pure, an immaculate lamb, for the feast would still be fulfilling—a secondhand messiah would carry her cross to Calvary: for most proxies are women, for most women are proxies for men. Under the permission of the proxy initiative even *nonbelievers,* such as my family, are willing to turn family into fodder; my blood is willing to turn my blood into water—and after more than *three years* of being an abomination my cooperation is expected, has always been expected, as I have always expected it of myself—despite failing to be available the first time. Yet had I, my love, made myself available, you might still be fighting for your life, hoping that your stay of execution isn't lifted, once the state finally attain the medicines they need to murder you—and me—which could've happened at any time; or maybe even dead by your own hand, after hearing about your nephew: Time for seconds, you might've said, to someone over the phone, before hanging up. I would've never known you. I would've never loved you. For as grisly as it is to admit, had my brother never mangled that woman, I wonder if I would've ever written to you, if I would've even had the urge to, for perhaps you were right, my love, perhaps I wrote to you to learn what it was like for you in order to learn what it *could* be like for myself—because now my mother has delivered her affront, and just as she knew that showing a ten-year-old girl the picture of her father's mistress and daughter would be kept a secret, without demanding it, so, too, will this secret be kept. For maybe the other reason, in addition to tradition, to the expectations of that shibboleth, maybe the other reason my mother had learned to love my brother more than me was because that mistress couldn't bear our father a son. But neither could our mother bear him another one. They both loved him, but he loved them both. Yet our mother had the money and the advantage and had lorded it over the mistress the best way she knew how: by furtively reminding our father of it, by having him carry his only sleeping insentient son from the car and into the house through childhood and manhood and marriage, until the day he died; so since the queen clownfish has survived the first male mate, naturally, the next biggest male will need to grow and take his place—so now *she* has to carry their son. And while my mother must've seen our interviews, my love, while she must've seen me on broadcast news siding with you, my lover my black lover, salting her wound with short sound bites of each renunciation of her son—three refusals before the end of our tour—she knows that she is the only one who knows otherwise, she knows that I would never tell you, until it is time . . . .

One cannot lie to oneself in the snow: there are times, the woman tells the man, who is next to her, trudging toward the river, when what is going on outside in the world is what is going on inside of me. Climate change is more evident in the wintertime, she tells him, on this crisp-air trek through the snowbound vale of the forest; farmers can no longer count on nature for any reliable means, planting season is earlier now, but in turn more crops are being destroyed by last-minute snowstorms or just unforeseen stretches of cold. We see the change. We have always seen it. We just never let it do what it needs to do to us: turn us into men and women and children of change, of action and not reaction. Our reaction is to do nothing. But it is only early January and they, the lovers, and everyone else and every thing still move between a sky so blue and an earth so white that they blind one to many things; ice and snow have covered the landscape for nearly two months now and the lovers and the provincials are growing more and more solitary in the subzero atmosphere, for some days it is just too insane to go outside, but if one must, the nose needs to be muffled; the woodpiles have dents in them and the woodstoves are working overtime, so that now the lovers and the provincials are all eying their split logs more carefully and counting more cords and space heaters per square foot to make sure they'll be covered in the cold stretches to come. Today, on their way to the river, there are outbursts of animal tracks everywhere, and the lovers following them see them as reviving reminders that not everything slows to solids in winter or sleeps, as spurts of verve, for rabbit and deer and predator trails spread so seemingly inexhaustibly that almost anyone can track their triumphs and defeats; so that on this crisp-air trek through the snowbound vale of the forest, the Black and Asian couple—as the provincials have come to know them—encounter something unusual in this wild grid of newly grown evergreens in the form of a puff of snow, for since they didn't see anything at first, they can't say for sure what has vanished—but now they can: a coywolf, a hybrid of the coyote and the wolf, a liminal being that is bounding up a wood-crested hill on the other side of a clearing when it turns to look back so that they're staring at each other for a bit, fixed, the lovers and the descendant of the *lupus*, the size of a shepherd dog, though the lovers cannot discern its black-tipped tail and reddish grizzled grey coat and face frozen in place, yet they stare, until it turns and ascends swiftly into the wood. The lovers stand in silence, then the man, concerned about a pack, wonders if they should return to the cabin. The woman tells the man that coywolves are not known for hunting humans, especially when they're afraid of them, and with an abundance of white-tailed deer about and being cunning and all-devouring, opportunistic, one can certainly see how they could sustain themselves on anything, from raccoons to rabbits to muskrats, from minks to moles to mice, from flora to fruit to refuse: they have the most plasticity of any other species up here; yet, since the lovers are not wearing their florescent orange vests over their double layers of winterwear and coywolves are now hunted throughout the season, they are overly cautious about nearby hunters missing their prey—and there is always that lurking racial concern, if only in the man's mind for the moment. It is getting colder and cloudier as they head back and on the way back fat plenteous snowflakes begin to fall, as they follow the still-visible foot traces of their past, for in the vale of the forest it is easy to get lost, everything looks like everything else every which way with the wispy fingers of flurries curling and curling *come here come here*, for the crystal skeletons of snow-covered deciduous trees and the shaggy white coats of evergreens are as far as the eye can see, which is why the lovers backpacked provisions—the vests escaping them—yet without the evidence of their movements in the snow, indeed, it would be difficult to navigate the return. In advance of the ascent—when they'll be laboring without words and stopping to catch breath, ungloved and mouthing and breathing on the tight beaks of their fingertips— the woman tells the man of another dream, a recurring one, and though she last experienced it seven or so months ago, it remains as intense—if not even more— as the recent one of her father, for it reminds her of her mother: In the dream of the black wolf, she says, I am frightened of it, not because it harms me but because it *refuses* to harm me; it does not maul me as I lay there on my side in the snow, my spine against the spine of an oak, a colossal sawtooth, with the snowfall covering me like a comforter. It waits. It is waiting for me to die. For even when the pack arrives, having spoored the alpha, they, too, wait. One is forever foolishly intrepid though and starts to inch forward, belly to snow with the snout shoveling it, throwing sly glances at the alpha to test it, until a snarl makes it retract into the pack. I lie there. The dream always ends there. The lovers reach the ascent to start their zigzagging climb toward the cabin, but only when they stop for a rest does the man decode the dream: The alpha is not showing pity but prudence, he says; it will not let the pack become con- taminated, it will not let them feed off your desire to die—for they are all one and the lowest of these wolves is you, in this disease state, the omega, and the highest is the alpha: it knows that it has to let this part of itself starve itself to death. Soon, after another rest, they reach the summit, and then come upon the cabin; after the sun has set, after they have settled and had supper, they decide to retire, but by lamplight, in a bedchamber of the double heart, the woman lies alone in her lover's bed, under a comforter. She touches the closed maroon curtains of his room, tempted by the dark window mirror, but she does not open them. The space heater is somewhat insufficient, but it is getting warmer when the lover returns, having stoked the fire in the furnace, fed it wood, for heat is now venting into the room. He gets into bed, sitting up against the headboard, and covers his lower half with the comforter as she spies the papers in his hand, folded in thirds; she fancies him having saved them from the furnace, the pages of one of his missives, but she knows he merely retrieved them from his desk in the rec room, for she recognizes her handwriting. Night is the best counsel, she says, so, forever foolishly intrepid, she glides a finger over his knuckle and on down the digit to make him slowly expose it, to unfold it and to hold it up to her face, for her to *inhale* herself, for her scent is still there in the mind but her slit hardly knows it, remembers it—it only remembers forgetting it, like a short piece of thread that had been passed through to the other side of a needle's eye—but with the black oblivion outside and the maroon curtains closed, like inverted labia aroused by a rub, drawing back the curtain of shame, the black oblivion *inside* now opens her inwardly: *Hold me open*, she always opened, for once more he is reading one of her missives, yet aloud and dearly to her. He will be conducting a séance with it. It is a memento, a reminder of an extraordinary discovery while he was reading it on the row, in a place where he had thought there were no new memories worth remembering, it was one of the few missives he was allowed to keep, for since it was written after those interviews—after which he had been beaten and humiliated then taken into solitary—it had yet to be written, thus confiscated, a missive he received last June only after he'd heard he was to be released, for since she did not want to burden him before she now felt that he needed to know what her memory had in store, in full, for them—though she had written the missive *months* before she sent it to him—for up until then he only knew that her son had been taken by that act of God, and man, but not about that act *during* the act, so that now so that now as her lover is reading this, as the voice of the missive is possessed by another's, or rather *dispossessed* of the body of the missive by another's, not the man's, *Open my mouth,* says the voice, *pull back the curtain of shame so that I may give back the name, for I can still smell the reek coming from it, my mouth of sex, that nautical stink which won't sink and be at peace in me and my belly for they—some shadowy they—say that it will take me the same sum of years as my son was to grieve him—five—and it has only been two and a half and so I cannot expect for him to sink and be at peace in me midway and perhaps he never will as he should, as I ought not to be, for I am a sibyl who is her own and only oracle now, a god who is her own and only atheist: I do not believe in myself, my love—so how can I believe in what I have done?* And as the man becomes the woman, metamorphosing into his new form, as this voice which is not *his* voice possesses or rather dispossesses hers from the body of the missive, the cabin, and the double black oblivions are all meshing and blending and metamorphosing into a sea and snow into saltwater and dark into daytime *for there will come a time,* it says, through her lover tonight, *when water will turn into blood* and soon she is smelling the saltwater and feeling the scalding summer sun kissing her suntan-lotioned face, as the soft fat frame of her sentient son, at the great brown-green girth of the earth, in the warm equatorial waters of the Atlantic, splashes between the support of her open arms, and then there is another, and another and another and there are seven other mothers right here at this great brown-green girth of the earth, all gathered together today beyond the broad break of a sandbar, and she is in her mid-thirties again over three years ago and is transatlantically in water as warm as bathwater on a fiery foreign beach on a spotless noonday today under a skin-darkening star, this American, this Asian American with her son, girdled by a dark indigenous assemblage of West African women with one as her guide, a friend of a friend, all glistening under this skin-darkening sun and holding *their* sentient children at the water's surface to show them how to stroke and float with their fat in the sea salt without any floatation device, for there are none on this non-touristy beach besides the coconuts attached to the fishermen's nets, for this serene broad break in the waves before the sandbar—in the hazel iris of these equatorial waters, with the soft eyes of distant storms being their moveable pupils—is a deceptively perfect place to play today, today she is not *other* here, she is not an Asian of Asia or an Asian of America, for though she is often referred to as *the American* by these women when speaking to one another—merely out of convenience, as a quick clarification of who is being spoken of—she has been unothered by these other mothers who are much much darker than her, on this primordial mega-continent, inside the hot equatorial junction of the dark blue thighs of all kinds all colors and creeds and where the custom is coastal and postcolonial and now allows for these women to partake of this newly unrestricted sector of the sea at this time of day and heat where they are *all* free to laugh and to bare skin and breasts and teeth under a sky and no male eye so blue with a sun so bold that it blinds one to many things, but only these *indigenous* women are the mothers of the human others, who are so dark that they are black and so black that they are blue and bright and as shiny as obsidian stones—a darkness that had long since birthed the many permutations of beauty across the globe to maybe one day eclipse the lunar surface itself—yes, obsidian yet malleable and rhythmical flesh and discourse and diatribe so that this whole world seems much more fuller than her own, elemental and alive and innate, only to have these thoughts parted and dispersed by a colossal cruise ship, anachronistically passing by like a penthouse gliding across the water, very long and multilayered, the building beneath it immersed—*Look! Look!*—some of the women are yelling in unison, in colonial or creole or tribal tongue—*The savages are waving! The savages are waving!*—with the American's guide, a friend of a friend, among them, and then they are all laughing and waving and shifting their hips without ever wondering why or if this great white ship is passing by too close, for they know *why*—it's a safari by boat, with their bare wet bosoms in the passengers' binoculars—and *if* has never really bothered them before—for ships rarely passed by in the past and so close and when they *did* the women were never permitted to be here and when they pass by *now* the women rarely are—the American's guide, another indigenous woman with her child, a son, has a face that bears the marks of her tribe and diatribes, a friend of a local friend who invited her here today, who speaks the colonial language of the vanquished so the American can understand her, a colonial language unlike the American's colonial language yet one the American has been speaking fluently for years, during her past wanderings across other countries that were once colonized by the same tongue, prior to her matrimony, prior to her pregnancy—despite the distaste of her family—but now the American's arms are under the soft plump torso of her horizontal son as a swell rolls across the surface, so that now she is standing on her toes with her chin barely above it and her heart in her throat, but her boy is steadily treading water without needing any help from her, laughing, as some of the other children and women are treading water as well, these women who are so much like the market women who are always smiling and doting on her boy, calling him *Buddha! Buddha!* while pinching his cheeks and who is kicking quite well with the water even higher now, dog paddling in a tight circle, saying *Mama Mama look!* with her treading water too, though now the water has leveled again, at her chest, and with her feet in the sand she continues to study her son, his strokes are easy, no wasted energy, and she remembers the saxophonist from the other night, from the hotel jazz club, the local who was trying to seduce her by offering to give her son swimming lessons in the hotel pool today, while her husband, another Asian American, was answering another critical call on his mobile cellular phone outside where it was less loud, as their son slept fifteen floors above them—where her husband is today, in the hotel room, taking a video conference call on his portable computer at the behest of his boss—for their local friend, their nanny, was watching their son last night, whose own child, her daughter, they'd find sleeping beside their son like a little wife—*For to them,* the voice says, through her lover tonight, *everyone is theirs, and I notice this mostly with yours, but not so much with mine, yet due to an appointment, fortuitously timed, the nanny couldn't come to the beach with her daughter that day*— and while her husband was still away, once she graciously declined the saxophonist's offer, he spoke and spoke about his music without ever taking a breath so that she had to stop him to ask him about his *sustained intensity*, about his *circular breathing*, and he said it was like being in the middle of a pool, like steadying yourself on the slope between the shallow end and the deep end, with your chin barely above the surface and your heart in your throat and while standing on the tips of your toes—that, he said, is sustained intensity, which equals ecstasy—but she is *glad* to have brought her son here instead of to a hotel pool today—*Salt is sacred*, says the voice, *the salt of the earth*—and now *Mama Mama look!* for she has been watching her son kicking and swimming while thinking of the saxophonist, yet only now is she really *seeing* him again, she embraces and kisses him, and then watches as the guide swims around them and her feet disappear, as her body goes vertical, for the sea is rapidly receding, and the American and her guide are both embracing their sons as the sea sucks them in, their legs, the receding seaweed catching at their ankles and the seabed sifting through their toes, for the sea itself seems to be coercing them to devolve or regress and return to some piscine way of being and breathing by way of this circular motion, this path of least resistance, for some of the other mothers are now shouting and rushing for their children, who are several feet away from them, for a massive wave—born of the cruise ship's colossal wake—surges and overwhelms and pummels them, breaking beyond the sandbar behind them, the massive uprush of the swash now feeding the massive backwash into the vast and foamy brine by way of the path of least resistance: the board break in the sandbar—so that now so that now they're *all* caught in the rip, the mothers and the children, moving at a velocity much much faster than any one of them could ever swim against, than *anyone* could ever swim against, trapped in this atrocious treadmill of water maybe fifty feet wide and who knows how long while shooting out to sea at several feet per second perhaps, so that whoever's at hand is in hand, as these mothers move farther and farther away from shore, grabbing and gripping hands and thinking and thanking God thank God or oh God oh God: my child is not my child—*and I remember I remember,* says the voice, *one of the sisters saying to me, one of the Buddhist nuns later on, that it was a selfless act, yet all I can see is my hand still holding onto that dear little hand for its dear little life, onto some other woman's son and not even thinking of mine at the time and this and this is what* gets *to me, that I wasn't even* thinking *of mine not so much of mine if only for a moment, but when I am I can do nothing but allow this rip to take me and the boy past the breaking point and out into its head and I can only hold up his head by having him on top of me and riding on my back, scanning the sea only to see some trying to swim against it, the rip, who'll get tired and be swept away anyway and then my eyes fall upon my guide, whose own eyes must've fallen on us, for though she's far away she is crying and screaming for me—no no not for me—for her child, she is screaming for her child who is half-limp and on my chest, yet once he hears her cry carrying across the surface he starts and struggles and I have to swim fast to catch him again when I lose hold of him—but then my heart stops: for my son is farther out; I can still hear her, the cries of that guide carrying across the water her horror, for though she's out of the rip she's out of her mind, yet treading water, she has gotten and is getting smaller as her son and I slip toward my son, and I will never stop hearing her— Bring me my boy! Bring me my boy!—and I will never ever stop seeing it, the sight of my son dog paddling—with no wasted energy—for where he is the rip seems to have ceased as he looks and looks straight at me—I know I know he's looking at me, I can feel it as far as he is from me—he wants he wants to get back to me as his own goddamn mother is moving away, swimming sideways and cursing herself, with one arm wrapped around another child while her other arm is stroking away, swimming parallel to the shore for some shadowy reason—for some shadowy they must've told her to do so, for she never knew to do so—for she must swim toward* someone *and she can't carry them both, so that once she's out of the rip she starts swimming toward the shore, toward the guide who's now swimming toward her too and once she meets her she can scarcely see her for already she is swimming back, childless and alone, but her shoulders are shot and her lungs are shit and she's gasping and thinking and thinking and gasping you are not going to drown you are not going to drown, but she can't see her son anywhere anymore, and she's not even sure if she's swimming to the right spot, for the life of the rip has stopped, yet she just keeps on toward the head of that dissipating stream of foam and dives under and then nothing but nothing but a stinging brown murk of aqua and bubbles and seaweed floating about, as her legs cramp and her arms end and her sinuses are shot with salt, the sharp pain at the base of her brain, as her mouth opens and closes and opens to swallow you are not going to drown you are not going to drown you are not going to drown....* Now, at night, in the dead of winter, she is lying in her lover's arms. His back is still against the headboard, but her missive is now scattered across the floor. She is crying. You can't come in me anymore, she says, you can't come in me anymore. I'm sorry I'm sorry, he says. I won't have another I won't have another. We won't have another we won't have another. And then her eyes rise, for her cheek was against his chest: We won't? We won't? We won't, my love, we won't .... The worst thing, she says, after a while, is thinking about what he must've thought when he saw me moving away. That I didn't want him. That I didn't love him. And then her lover says to her, very softly: At that moment, not any other, you had a life in your hands. That's what one of the sisters said to me, she says, one of the Buddhist nuns, and that not saving my son was a selfless act. I thought about that, about them, about becoming one of them. Yet: I would've had to disrobe to love you. I would disrobe to love you .... We had to focus on one pant leg at a time, she continues, my husband and I. He stayed beside me for six months afterward, when my own family would not, throughout the insane asylums of the recovery resorts, throughout the drinking. I could've lied and said that I didn't see him, our son—but that would've been unbearable. We have the right to be angry, he said, but it is not our duty. But before he left me, You

67

are not a walking reminder, he said to me, as much as I am a walking reproach—and can't help it. I want so badly to but can't help it: you would do it the same. And then I looked at him, for I couldn't look at him until then, and he looked away: I am a mirror, I said, and men don't like what they see in me. But we continued to have sex for a time, and now he has long since remarried and has his twins, a boy and a girl—which made me relapse when I heard about it: I *wanted* to be alone, you see, but I wanted him to be alone with me. God, what awful conduits we are, you and I: two disconnected cords trying to retain their identities, still believing they are holding some past electricity—and the only reason we are not drinking too much now, my love, is because of the forest; we really don't need to have spirits in the house. Even the coroner, a man obsessed with them, had said it, that death is a myth. I kept coming to see him, that blue-black man in the morgue, with his white crown and his silver flask and his steely grey beard, even though he never sent for my husband or me: I was a zombie, you see, so I knew where I ought to be; we stayed in that country for a week, my husband and I, and I couldn't sleep, I couldn't eat—all those things moving around down there and just nibbling and nibbling away—I was a vitamin-deficient organism existing in the lavishness of a touristy establishment, contemplating flight from the fifteenth floor—yet I *still* don't know why I never did it—feeling the acute caress of a phantom limb in the darkness of a hotel room—that agony we, the affluent, always hypothesize about between martinis—but the body would never be found; three children had died on that day and they only found two, another boy and a girl—and I couldn't even find a comfort in this, in this sick perversity: that somewhere in that dry and loud and dusty city two other women were ripping their wombs out and wrapping them around their heads to carry the ghosts of their dead around like buckets of water from the river; and the only reason why I wasn't among them—I should've been among them, the children—was because of a fisherman who had fished me out, right after I swam back out, the one who saw the wave wipe us out, the voyeur; he retrieved me and revived me as the warm water on my bare breasts, under that skin-darkening sun, evaporated quicker than I could wrap my head around the matter. You are a miracle, the coroner said. Yet I felt and still feel that nature does not and *cannot* absorb this variety of raw and invisible anger, it can only provide a protective covering to numb it—for you will *always* be conscientious of the supreme and irrefutable fact that it didn't need to happen. That is the rack. But you could've *never* let that other child go, the coroner said to me, during my last visit, for he was a comfort to me, for he would always say, Let me see, whenever he spoke to me—as *you* would say to me. Let me see. As if I were a body without a murderer. Or rather: as if I were a murderer without a body. Maybe we kept each other company, because he was always surrounded by spirits that only spoke in terms of the present, like amnesiacs, who still believed in the delusions of their egos so deeply that—even beyond matter—their minds still moved around: But to be honest, he said, before taking a swig from his flask, I would rather be calm than right . . . .

Mid-January: a winter thaw, a skein of wild geese. Old women and men say, This has always been. The snow's melting reveals frozen mud and lifeless yellow grass, and for a week or two winter will taste its imminent end. A lover is misled, believing in a premature spring, as the other dons a pashmina of gloom, for like the provincials she knows it won't last: the thaw is nature's stay, a reprieve from the cold and the snow in the dark, and yet again the snow and the cold will come: a man does not wipe away the frost that rimes his beard. A lover is sick, daylight crawls and the crows comfort him; the crows: their knowledge of the beneficent face—yet thousands avoid the men who mark and pellet them; whole migratory patterns are known to shift and change shapes for a face, as their offspring assimilate the datum; the crows are the cognitive equals of the ancestors of these men, the primates of the skies, whose astuteness affords them the capacity to fashion tools to fetch foods; now a lover is feeding them, nurturing them, while watching through the bedroom eyes of his windows, but then a caw, another and another, and the crows have scattered: after gestating in his stomach, the black silken bird of sickness had showed itself first in the looseness of his bowel movements, then rose and nested in his thorax, his throat, ripping it raw, and is congesting his sinuses—so that his caws now extrude it into a tissue. He had thought that the drastic shift in temperature had just given him a cold. But no. Still, even this can be a benefit. Crisis could bring clarity. Once the mind can no longer tolerate a single negative deadbolt the door will swing wide open and some lesser muscles will contract to make every hair on the back of your neck applaud. No more aphorisms. No more verses. You will fall into an awareness so deep that it will almost be satanic—luciferous—for this will surely be the benediction of the shining serpent: duality is the belief in singularity, singularity is the belief in duality. Every opposite contains its own opposite. Like a winter thaw. Old women and men say, This has always been. But no. Not a cold: this influenza—these chills and aches and headaches. He thinks his feet must look so swollen and lonesome on this shaggy warm rug right now, at night, as he sits on the side of his bed, in his thermals, readying himself to shuffle through the darkness and the grogginess again to urinate into a hole, his commode, and then over and over again later, for he would rather not turn on the lights, for his diurnal vision has shifted to the nocturnal and his thoughts from soma to soul at dusk, for daylight can be unfordable when you are ill and incapacitated under the sun's daily vigor, so one must mostly sleep through the current of its events. But now the nightcrow is wide awake, alone, with his lover so sad and awkward in her own room that she's wide awake as well, having stirred, moving above him, painfully wanting to nurse him—for he *requested* this, this aloneness; not because he doesn't want to infect her— *she* infected *him* while *he* was nursing *her*—but because he has not found a way to allow himself to be touched in times of intense healing, because when a scourge is running its course it has to run its course and one must fast from any somatic contact, from any negative thought, if one is to see anything lucidly, because a single touch could disconcert him and could cause him to become irritable and excitable and incapable of distinguishing between the rash of his own feelings and the rash of hers, as *she* would be unable to distinguish hers from *his*—even that fear of his, that childhood fear of bumps and blisters and scabby lesions, all over his mind all over his body, on the mucous membranes around his eyes and anus, from that episode of chicken pox. No. Misery doesn't need any company. Misery has its own. Right now he is that same dejected child with chicken pox, chastened by chicken pox, self-born in self-pity, grotesque again; whereas he would later learn to soothe this sadness in childhood by intermittently pretending to be mentally *slow* when he was alone, pitiable and pure, in order to conjure a certain quantum of compassion for himself while rocking back-and-forth on the side of his bed and staring into space with his head tilted and fingers clenched in a fist as if clutching a swing, or shuffling through the darkness in daylight or night, with those fingers now fidgeting viciously; even then, he wonders again, for he has thought about it before, many times before: had he been in tune with his unborn nephew? foreknown him? aped him before he was even here to ape? But this childish behavior would never surface in his mind as an act of self-compassion until mid-January of last year, during a witching of shingles in prison, and today is the first anniversary of that attack, that reactivation of the chicken pox virus that has happened too early in his life, according to the medical consensus, in his early forties instead of in his early fifties, for perhaps that shingles attack occurred because he had killed a countless number of mosquitoes the summer before, for some believers in Blood Law, that indigenous concept of reparation or retribution, don't recognize degrees of killing, since they believe even the ghosts of insects—whose bodies are always unavoidably trampled—can infect you with infirmities, if no appeasements are made—and he felt that he was not so much culpable as accountable. Crisis can bring clarity. But only if one's not attached to the outcome. For before that shingles attack, during the preceding summer, he had a foreboding experience, a premonition, an anguish so tortuous and debilitating that he *knew* it was very real, that that psychic pain must have—and indeed did—come from far beyond his imagination, that *the thing* that was causing the psychic pain seemed to have happened but had *yet* to happen—and without him knowing what the thing would be or how it would happen or to whom it would happen—for in the crucible of his cell that mosquito summer, with the central air conditioning malfunctioning, he had cried in utter defeat in utter despair, not because of the plague of mosquitoes that were exsanguinating him to the point that his hands were so turgid and tight that his fingers looked like sausage links, not because of the walls that were abstract triptychs of blood splotches from all the tiny pulverized bodies, not because of his inability to stay still long enough to sleep due to the stylets sucking his eyelids avidly—for colonies were breeding in the commodes of the empty adjacent cells of those self-castrated lovers—and not because he had to sleep either fully clothed and boil in his own juices or nude to cool off and be a feast—no, none of these, or not *just* because of these—but because of the pang of the premonition: in that mosquito summer, without knowing it, he was feeling what he *would* feel after receiving a phone call from his sister that upcoming winter, orchestrated by the chaplain. So when that winter came, when he was holding that receiver to his ear, shackled with shingles, that same tortuous and debilitating pain returned to him from that summer before: his nephew had sat down on the floor, and hung himself . . . . Yes, despite the fact that he was suffering for his nephew, that same tortuous and debilitating pain was not so much from the grief but from the guilt—from his perceived accountability—because during that shingles attack, during the painful soreness and itching due to the bumps and blisters and scabby lesions all over the right side of his face and eyelid and parts of his scalp— possibly precipitated by the ghosts of those mosquitoes, but most likely due to the sapped immune system and the stress from his looming execution, which *still* needed to happen and could have happened at any time—after living in a cell between two madmen for too long, he was so sad and senseless that he had to be sent to the psychiatric unit, under a suicide watch. Normally, having the option of suicide can give a person the *release* they really need to endure, but since the sentence could no longer be reverted to the nephew now—had the *uncle* hung himself—since the evidence of his nephew's innocence seemed so inaccessible, there seemed to be no *reason* for him to stay: the governor had given him that stay only after two months in, possibly due to the case's publicity, the public outcry, but most likely due to the state's inability to attain the medicines it uses for executions—for the governor could've been telling the truth; most people aren't aware that such a postponement might be possible, and for so long, for the ability to attain the medicines would become increasingly difficult, outlasting the uncle's total time on the row: two years and three months and three days; distribution restrictions have been put into place by many pharmaceutical companies across the country, fighting the misuse of their medicines, so it is stated, and export regulations have been instituted by many across the world— though the death penalty states in this country are still seeking to expand their secrecy statutes, to cover participating companies. But even despite his perceived accountability, for the uncle, there was just no reason to stay. Because before the nephew's Miranda rights were waived (or before they were never even read to him), before those two detectives fed the facts to the confused and exhausted mind of the boy in the twenty-two-year-old body (without his counsel present), before the tongue attached to his mind would parrot the facts as a confession (a false confession), there had been that mentally defective black boy whom he had horribly failed, that fatherless little boy who was forever fated to become that backward black man in a foreboding body, who after becoming that five-foot-ten, two-hundred-and-ten-pound man had once more found himself fatherless and alone and without suitable associates to guide him, or even the basic sociability to acquire them, as his mother—throughout the boy's later life— worked long hours through the wee hours as a night nurse, leaving this innocent to befriend *unsuitable* associates, who were always much younger in age and street-smart and much more manipulative than him, and who would later lead him to the night of his first and only arrest, and then to his first and only conviction: guilty by association. All of which could've been avoided had the uncle, the only available father figure in the boy's life, taken the initiative to rear him right when he really needed him: guilty by *dis*association. Yes, the uncle may have been there after the prognosis, he may have been there throughout the boy's childhood, but for over a decade, throughout the boy's pre-teen and teenage years, he had lived across the country, working in the educational system so that he could write in seclusion over the summers, in hopes that he might one day secure a livelihood as an author and a professor; but a few years before the arrest, when he returned to the city of his birth in the northeast— sickened by being harassed by the police for being black in the northwest—the boy had the body of a man—and the uncle's ambition hadn't come to fruition. But *had* it or had *he* been reborn as a parent or as a spouse or both, instead of, or as well as, an author of efficacious essays, would he have taken the initiative? Would *anyone* have who had been reborn as a parent or as a spouse or both, instead of, or as well as, an author of efficacious essays? He has often thought about it. No, he now thinks, sitting on the side of his bed: I am *not* responsible. Or at least I am not the only one. For *had* he raised his nephew right when he really needed him and not just left him as the boy's father had left him before the boy was even born—as the uncle's father had left *him* and his sister, the boy's mother—given the world as it was and still is, given their income and color and the boy's condition, maybe the outcome would've still been the same: maybe the nephew would've found the same or similar associates who would've still had him out there gallivanting at night, out of poverty and monotony, and he might've still been ill-fated enough to find himself in that bodega or some other bodega on that same night or some other night as a nearby homicide (as if these inner city homicides are typically so uncommon or occur so far apart from one another that one might avoid their proximity), maybe those underage associates, who are still too young today to purchase malt liquor and beer (but old enough to be executed if warranted), would've still been able to manipulate that much older innocent to purchase malt liquor and beer for them—as they usually would've been able to do—while they stealthily relieved the establishment of a few choice items, maybe once he was rounded up with several other men fitting the same and standard description he would've still been broken under duress, maybe his reasoning would've still been compromised by mental retardation, by confusion and fear and brute force, by alcohol, after being held in a loud and lively holding cell—where blacks like him and unlike him are often deposited by the police, a barracoon that stirred and stewed and deprived him of some necessary sleep—maybe he, being an innocent, would've still felt so sinful and reprehensible for aiding in the theft of those many choice items that he would've still thought that the *thefts*—not anything else—were why the detectives were browbeating and beating him, maybe he would've still felt so confused that he would've confessed and scribbled his name so childishly at the bottom of a typed confession that he would've had to slowly and legibly sign it again: a confession that was never read to him. Yes, even had he, the uncle, stayed and raised his nephew right when he really needed him, perhaps he would have *still* grown up to have this happen to him, or something similar to this, perhaps he would've *still* confessed to something that was drastically different than what he *thought* he was being accused of, and—aided by the coerced testimonies of his underage associates, all of whom with infractions already and fearful of being implicated in a murder— would've *still* been convicted. The judge, a hanging judge, a black man known to be racially biased against blacks, had allowed the confession to be heard, to sway the jury, a mostly white jury—for after the defense had challenged its admissibility, due to the unread Miranda rights and the lack of present counsel, the judge had said that he *believed* the detectives' testimonies, that the defendant's rights *were* read to him, and that the defendant *did* state that he understood and waived them and was now not telling the truth, or just couldn't recall it. For memory does play its tricks. Even the uncle would wonder if the nephew *knew* what he was confessing to—after a while—but had forgotten it after being placed inside a single cell as promised, after some much-needed rest, after sobering up. Maybe, before he awoke, he had fallen back on his default sense of remorse, on the wearing guilt of those thefts, for his account of what had happened after the arrest and during that long night of detainment under duress seemed more like a mixture of conjecture and coercion than fact. Maybe, before he fell back on that default, maybe those two detectives with their interrogation techniques had inculcated the crime in his head. Maybe they just told him and told him what he did and how he did it, subtly at first, and then forcefully and physically and then ever so sweetly over a few of his choice snacks and drinks that—with his already subpar processing state, not to mention his being compromised by confusion and fear and brute force, by alcohol and lack of rest—he might've *thought* that he had done it, after hours and hours of being told that he did it—at least for a while, until after some much-needed rest. There is no way to know. For video and audio recordings during interrogations are not required by the state (as video and audio recordings are not required on the row). But whether the nephew knew or didn't know what he was confessing to at the time, whether he momentarily thought that he had committed the crime or not, he *definitely* did not and could not understand that a white man, a minister, had been murdered—for no one is on death row for killing a black, though blacks disproportionately populate the cells—near the same bodega he and his associates had left an hour earlier that night. Regardless, in his defense, his court-appointed attorney had told the jury that he had confessed to the crime because he was tired and confused and scared, and was getting even more tired and confused and scared, and he thought that maybe if he just believed what they wanted him to believe and said what they wanted him to say and signed what they wanted him to sign he would be able to go home and eat and sleep and be awakened by his mother in the morning from this very torrid nightmare, and be told that everything was not as bad as he had dreamt it, but only as bad as he had left it, before closing his eyes again . . . . Behind the cabin, in the wee hours, in the cold fresh air of winter thaw, his freezing bare feet, he thinks, must look so sad and swollen on this frosty dead sward right now; he cannot stop peeing, several times tonight, always inside, so now he needs to nitrogenize the turf, to be energized, to be invigorated by the elements. Night is the best counsel. But now he is wondering about his prostate and kidneys, about being in his early forties. Life, he says, on this springy turf, reaching down into his heart and grabbing the grubs and the dirt and all the foul words that could be shouted into the open air are like sprouts shooting wildly from his fist; and with the clouds thickly wrapped around the wound of the moon, to the unenlightened eye, the darkness would seem so absolute that it would be like being in a bottle of ink. But with his nocturnal vision still active, his having emerged from the unlit cabin, on this frosty dead sward that leads down into a bottomless abyss, the vale of the forest, he can still see just a little bit of everything in front of him, unafraid and free, for it is only when you turn on a flashlight that the forest becomes terrifying, when you can only see what is born and bred behind your eyes and nothing more—and then all around you *you* are untrue; for it was only a year ago when he was using his mind like a flashlight inside of a white blood cell at night, shackled with shingles, and soon to be in a psychiatric cell, looking limitedly into the future with a fading beam of hope—for hope is conflict—endlessly and maddeningly awaiting the release of an article of clothing that could graciously hold the biological evidence and the prints of the *true* murderer of the white minister in this state that had wanted to murder a young innocent with a mental deficiency instead—for the state had never conceded the veracity of the nephew's deficiency—in this state that had adopted an initiative as egregious as—if not worse than—the death penalty itself; for to try to instill a selfless concern for others in a claimed killer by *killing* one of their closest relations is insane and what drove *me* insane, he thinks, as if he were writing, as if he were preparing to write these essayistic thoughts, despite the fact that I was sacrificing myself for my nephew, an *innocent*, the guilt and the loneliness and the persecution he had to endure as an idiot and a murderer and a coward, during and after his confinement, had ultimately ended him anyway. The uncle makes a small sound and touches his face. He has gone back inside and is wiping his eyes on the hem of his thermal undershirt. He puts on his woolen socks, sits on his bed, and begins rocking back-and-forth, staring into his space. Moments pass. Yet what roused me, he thinks, what roused me from my lunacy was the superabsurdity that my nephew's suicide wouldn't even save me: I still needed to seek clemency, I still needed my sister and my lover and my new defense attorney—for that clumsy court-appointed attorney had long since been dismissed—to continue to rally the public outcry to recover the very article of clothing that I needed to have tested, for after I was once more deemed competent and capable of comprehending the crime's connection to the punishment (for the condemned cannot be killed unless they have a rational comprehension of the crime and its connection to the punishment), after the psychiatrist was done with me, with a series of injections this proxy for the malady of society would still need to be anesthetized and paralyzed to be neutralized by the *body* of this society: so that white blood cell could contain another malady. Many think it is gratuitous, if not horrendous. Cruel, if not criminal. Yet the progenitor and the proponents of the initiative, that right-left religious sect (who had outnumbered the opponents at the voting booths again), maintain that it's a *safeguard* against a sort of *recidivism* (two dubious words)—for if *one* proxy-freed offender's suicide were to save his proxy, then what would prevent others from doing the same? What would prevent them from undermining this system of justice? of reformation? from cheating the God-fearing family of the victim by escaping the punishment of guilt and grief and quite possibly the power of grace? Executing their proxies could deter *future* proxy-freed offenders from following suit. Yet I have to wonder, he thinks, organizing his thoughts before writing them, how can you save an innocent by doing him wrong? And even if saving me by suicide was my nephew's intent—he didn't leave a note—would this not be—and it's tortuous and debilitating to admit it—an altruistic act? Isn't *this* the initiative's intent, for him to commit some altruistic act? For despite the safeguard, he thinks, this is the *second* time in the five initiative states, the two northeastern and the three Midwestern states, in the initiative's eleven years, that a proxy-freed offender has committed suicide out of guilt and grief and quite possibly out of a false belief that it would free his proxy—for that *first* suicide also didn't leave a note. Yes, there have only been *two* suicides, but proxy cases are rare: ten in total. Yet, according to the progenitor and the proponents of the initiative, even *if* the suicides were altruistic, given that these proxy-freed offenders were once convicted of first-degree murder, they'd be recidivist as well. The progenitor and the proponents of the initiative have all stated—despite this being a society allegedly free of state religion—that suicide is a sin: self-murder; and as far as freeing their proxies, even *without* the safeguard, they say the situation is the same as if those proxy-freed offenders had killed themselves on the row: suicide would not have pardoned them posthumously—so why should it pardon the proxies? A proxy is condemned for the *crime*, not the criminal, the *sin*, not the sinner—for if the *proxy* had suicided instead, indeed, the sentence would simply revert to the proxy-freed offender—a sister safeguard—for the proxy-freed offender is on parole and not allowed to leave the state, let alone the country (an absconder would be caught and executed too), until either after the execution or the pardon of the proxy (for there has never been an exoneration until now). According to that media mogul–politician, that billionaire who had conceived the initiative, it is supposed to *encourage a more progressive humanitarianism by way of its magnanimous inception*—but this is fucking insane! The hypocrisy is maddening! Instead of providing a clause that would pardon proxies for proxy-freed suicides—at least—that madman instituted the opposite—so that that *one* proxy in the past, that woman, that meaningless martyr, was crucified for a safeguard. Maybe her stepson and my nephew had killed themselves without the thought of freeing anyone other *than* themselves? Regardless, I, too, would be crucified for a safeguard, for this obsession to kill. Subconsciously, inside that psychiatric cell, this superabsurdity must've superseded the madness, or maybe the two had just canceled each other out or just clashed together and roused me, brought me back to my senses, a crisis of clarity—for it seemed as if I just sat up and said that I cannot defend myself, or maybe I just thought about it, if I'm screaming at phantoms and flinging my feces. Insanity is like humility. True humility does not know itself—so one can never know when it is happening to them. There is no awareness of the experience. Just the experience. But one can certainly know when it is absent . . . . A caw. The nightcrow caws. Catarrh in the dark. From his bed, from his sinuses, he is extruding mucus into a tissue—and now snorting and gagging on it. The scourge is running its course. It cannot be stopped. Only its ravages on the body can be abated by bad medicines, by pharmaceuticals—which are really quite nice now. He caws, again and again, and then quiets himself, listening, yet only a creak comes from the cabin, unprovoked by a foot. Yes, insanity, though it is hard to prove, would have kept him alive without that stay of execution, which would've been lifted after the state attained the medicines to murder him, but maybe subconsciously he *knew* he needed to be sane, he needed to honor his nephew, he needed to fight, he needed to assist his sister in the posthumous exculpation of her son by generating more public support, by continuing to do interviews, by continuing to write—for if you cannot articulate the pain of those who can no longer articulate it for themselves, if they ever could, after a while, it is as though the pain had never been born or borne. Still, this exculpation could've came posthumously for the *both* of them: two for the price of one. Yes, two niggers for the price of one. That was what they must've thought and still must think, the right, the opponents *and* the proponents of the initiative, who may believe that first-degree murderers should be executed, but also that their parents or guardians are just as culpable and accountable as them—especially if they're red or black or brown. Maybe this was why they didn't put up much of a fight against the initiative in the first place, and why they're still not doing much about it today, as it expands from five states to the other twenty-five death penalty states? Maybe it's because of that precise and cynical understanding that not too many people would sacrifice themselves for a first-degree murderer in the family, and would wait maybe months and months in a cell before dying? So why not just leave it alone? Maybe it's because its progenitor is a media mogul–politician, a billionaire, with the power and the prestige to persuade? Or maybe they just truly believe in it now? No, the *true* opposition to the initiative is coming from the left, from the opponents to the death penalty period, for *capital punishment is the most premeditated of murders, to which no criminal's deed, however calculated, can be compared; for there to be an equivalency the death penalty would have to punish a criminal who had warned his victim of the date at which he would inflict a horrible death on him, and who from that moment onward had confined him at his mercy for months; such a monster is not encountered in private life.* Still, some proponents of the death penalty, that right-left religious sect, believe that the proxy initiative could be beneficial to both parties, but that these parties are not political parties: it could be a restoration of grace through the faith for the offender and their family, and a step toward healing and forgiveness for the family of the victim. Yet, though the media assists in the spreading of these beliefs, with this somewhat recent suicide—along with that first one and the many judicial errors in capital cases in general—the initiative has once more backfired and galvanized another polarized debate. But *has* it backfired? *Is* the initiative a failure? For despite the hardships of prejudice and unemployment at first, after each of their respective conversions, eight out of the ten proxy-freed offenders have not only reformed but are now spreading the Good Word throughout the world—for they are *all* now sponsored by affluent church affiliates of that right-left religious sect. Even this somewhat recent suicide and the debate itself still makes for great media demand—for the proxy initiative conceals and has concealed from its conception an obsession *obliged* by mass communication: an unhealthy preoccupation with a rite of sacrifice as dark as the River Styx. For that right-left proposition begun by that media mogul–politician had been abominably born from a twisted interpretation of the Scriptures: *Just as the Lord Father had felt fit,* he once said, during a public address, covered and quoted by his media, *to allow His Holy Son to be substituted for a capital criminal called Barabbas—another son of the Father—so should we allow a child of God—at the discretion of the ones most offended by the offense—to rise and redeem a capital criminal in the family. For who knows what became of Barabbas? Who knows what quiet instrument of benevolence he may have become once reformed by this ultimate service? For it is hard for thee to kick against the pricks! Look at Saul, who became Paul, who aided in the murder of many Christians before becoming a Christian himself! For I, too, was a killer of innocents once, fallaciously, many years ago in war—you've all heard about it—and while I was a prisoner of war I was saved by an enemy officer, who against my will had allowed a devoted brother-in-arms to volunteer to die in his superior's place—for someone had to die. Now look at what I've become! Look at all the people around the world—in the very country I was once at war with—that I've been able to aid. For though that brother-in-arms was not without sin, the feast was still fulfilling—for the Lord God works in mysterious ways! And though I would never claim to know the great pain of the families of the slain, nor of the families of the slayers, I still want to offer this great spirit of service to them—for the greater good of us all!...* Or is it? For the greater good of us all. Couldn't it just be some tasteless social experiment, born out of some lust for media fodder? Or out of some madness that only the affluent can afford? Or is it simply a distraction from—or even a *catapult* into—something more politically insidious? For this madman has already campaigned for the governorship of the first state that adopted his initiative, his home Midwestern state, and has since devastatingly succeeded. Maybe a higher office is to come? Yet despite the claims of goodwill, this initiative is nothing more than an amendment to the capital constitution of five American states. Even the daughter of the murdered white minister is against it—this penalty of death by the state—*for you will not kill in my name,* she said, during a public address, and the media covered and quoted her saying that *what the world needs is* not *someone who can walk across water, who can heal the sick, who can resurrect the dead, but someone who can* forgive—

despite the tremendous pain. For make no mistake: I am in
tremendous pain. Yet I do not consider myself to be better or
nobler than anyone else who is under such dolor and unable
to do the same. I simply cannot justify murder—any
murder. But I, too, am human. For after the trial an officer
had asked me, if I had a gun, if I were there, would I have
used it to save my father? I told him I might have. But to
sin *means* to miss the mark—*and there is nothing more*
calamitous than a white woman in fear. For make no
mistake, no matter what we live through, in this offense,
our prejudices will always survive. Our prejudices will
always survive. A creak. Another and another. For the
beloved is moving above. The door facing the stairs is
shut, but there is no light on under it: she must be
using her *own* natural night sight or the bathroom
nightlight. The nightcrow listens to her stream, and
then to the rush of centripetal water. He follows her
footsteps back to the threshold of her room, but instead
of passing over they pause, and then creak across the
floorboards to the stairhead, pausing again: he imagines
her looking down from black to black and can see that
she is looking as indecisive as her steps: her disheveled
hair is growing fast, yet it is still short and beneath her
standards; she wants to shave it, yet wants it long; the
warm junctional wrinkles beneath her pajamas and
panties she hopes to have hard-pressed, ironed out, and
yet she also wants them to stay tucked away. The nightcrow caws. Again and again. And then quiets himself.
A creak. Another and another. And then the footsteps
stop: her door remains ajar . . . .

M ost of the families of the victims who had allowed the proxy option were headed by a female, and if it wasn't for the man, every one of the proxies who came forth would've been female as well, for the daughter of the murdered white minister had allowed the mother of the murderer to come forth first—though the daughter had always been against it, this pursuance of the capital sentence. The state was not acting on her behalf. It was election year and the politics of the prosecutor (who has since become the city district attorney), the locale of the crime (a county fanatical for *lex talionis*), and the class and the race of the two parties involved (a white work-ing-class victim and a poor black perpetrator) had all *demanded* the pursuance of the capital sentence; but after the sentencing hearing, visibly distraught, the daughter of the murdered white minister had admitted to the media that she was not so sure that the defendant was even guilty, and had been inclined to believe in his mental deficiency, which had been *unrecognized* by the judge, and could not stand the state putting *anyone*, let alone someone like this, to death, a man-child; and she was so shamefully and dreadfully conflicted that in direct opposition to her pacifist's belief and to the prosecutor's intent—who, despite being an implacable representative of the local government, had still been legally obligated to present to her a rightful alternative—while still mourning the recent death of her father, as an unthinkable *kindness* she had allowed the proxy option after looking into the wretched face of the mother of the man-child in question, who had asked to take it that day in court. No, the brother said to the sister—the younger of the two, right after the sentencing hearing, for the sister would've had the whole week to be sure—that boy will die if you do. That boy will die if I don't. I'll take it. No, she said. I'm how, he said, but *you* get *me* out. I have faith you'll get me out. For they both knew that that man-child in question—given the recent incident in the county jail complex—was not strong enough to survive another *month* locked up alone let alone on *the row* and for the years and years or *decades* it could take for him to simply see the end of his appeals—not many men are—yet, though the younger brother of the man-child's mother had already made up his mind, prepped himself for this feared result, as part of the procedure he still had a whole week and the week went very slowly, surreally, for after the sentencing hearing, after visiting the man-child who was still being detained in the county jail complex, after settling some affairs and saying a few farewells, the rest of his week was spent sitting in a seaside inn or in a lighthouse over two hundred miles away or swimming in the ocean—for the need to be alone was great—while during each swim he considered swimming farther and farther out from shore forlorn and unfit to bring himself to be touched by *any* woman so as not to be touched by *every* woman who had ever really loved him—for just as he has never been able to allow himself to be touched in times of intense healing only *now* has he been able to allow himself to be healed in times of intense touching—so since he had been chaste for a time to focus on his affairs, his vocation, he decided to remain untouched; it was the drive to the courthouse that went very quickly, not the week, no matter how slowly he drove himself and his sister in her sedan, smelling the sweet foreign foods of a nearby festival, recording the rows and rows of homes in his mind and then *regretting* not having had a woman over the week, for it was a sunny sad day driving beside his sister, his older sister, trying not to glance at her breasts that were unusually youthful and full for her age and not just emergent as they once were in her youth, and she asked him if he wanted her to drive when she noticed him sitting at yet another green light and he said no not now and instead of sitting behind her steering wheel he was soon sitting behind her son after he'd been brought out in hand-cuffs and leg-irons with a tether chain to sit beside his attorney, in that courtroom where his nephew was now rocking back-and-forth in his chair unconsciously as he, the uncle, used to consciously do as a child— right after his and his sister's nana had died, and then once more as a man after their mother had died, both women from cancer in the breast—the nephew was neither wearing an orange one-piece jumpsuit as he had at the sentencing hearing nor one of the two suits he had been given by the uncle for the trial, no, he was wearing the street clothes he had been arrested in and you could tell he had been crying, his eyes red and swollen: the day after the sentencing hearing, in the county jail complex, his uncle had come alone to visit him and to tell him of his decision—for he was allowed only one visitor a day and his mother was to visit him the next—but how could the nephew really have registered that this would be the last time that he and his uncle would play prisoner and visitor respectively, before the swap, in spite of the fact that his uncle had made it quite clear to him that, despite what was said at the sentencing hearing, his mother would *not* be taking his place, but would be taking him home? The nephew was still reeling from the verdict, for in this special visiting room of the county jail complex, on one side of a visiting booth with shatterproof glass, a guard standing outside the steel door behind him, the nephew had neither any wits nor breath to say anything at first, so over a slim desk he just sat there holding his head in one hand, propped up on the elbow, while holding the phone receiver in the other, after his *uncle's* breath had stopped flowing over his vocal cords—after the wind, the nephew imagined, had stopped blowing over the sunlit leaves outside—the airstream no longer vibrating the thin tissue and generating the chatter transferred through the receiver: silence was now as simple and complex as the mechanics of communication; but after a while the nephew's breath began flowing over his *own* vocal cords, generating What I do what I do? and then the uncle's breath began flowing over his again, saying It's alright it's alright I'm gonna make it alright, but then the nephew didn't know what to say again, for he just wanted to go home and eat and sleep and be awakened by his mother in the morning from this very torrid nightmare, and be told that everything was not as bad as he had dreamt it, but was only as bad as he had left it (yet after registering the reality, over the same receiver the next day, he would be told by his court-appointed attorney that he had no say-so in the situation, being found guilty, that he was powerless to refuse *any* proxy—for this would be part of the punishment now: the punishment of freedom). I tried real hard, said the nephew to the uncle, real hard, and then he started to sob. He was not referring to the test *of* his life but *for* his life, for since the highest court in the country had recently deemed it unconstitutional to execute a person with a mental deficiency, before the trial, the same intelligence quotient test had been given to him twice—for he had never been tested before. The first was given by the defense, by a psychologist, and he clearly scored within the classification of mental retardation; but the second was given by the prosecution, by a different psychologist, and he scored just above it, so since this score was higher than the first—discounting for *the practice effect*—the prosecution had accused the defendant of malingering, of intending to score low the first time. Moreover, it was argued that he was *not* a boy in a man's body, as the defense had stated, but a super-predator of the streets, with the intelligence to beguile storeowners on multiple occasions, as his underage associates stole for him, as they would attest to on the stand. The judge rendered his decision: the defendant was *not* sufficiently disabled to merit clemency from the capital penalty. Everyone was devastated. The mother and the uncle and the court-appointed attorney. But the defendant was proud: I did the best I could. So that now, growing more and more despondent in the special visiting room of the county jail complex, behind the glass, the nephew began talking about his previous accommodations, about the cell he was in before he was moved into this stabilization unit, before he was moved into this new mental health unit designed for surveilling prisoners considered to be a threat to themselves or to others, began speaking about a cell similar to the cell—if not the same cell—where *the uncle* would be held before the transfer: that previous cell, with its feed slot locked from the outside, had no bars no sun no cellmate, just a closet of a room with a twin bed and a toilet-sink and two unbreakable windows, one looking out onto the back of another grey building and sheeted with rusty metal mesh while the other on the steel door faced another across the corridor, beyond which that previous prisoner, so he was told, had hung himself. And he couldn't get it out of his head, the nephew, after some dulcet voice from the ventilation vent spoke about it, from that first night to two weeks later he would wonder what that torso across the corridor and behind the window of that opposite steel door must've looked like, swaying and swaying, even *after* he had figured it out, the truth—for he would *still* believe in this entrenched mental image—he would wonder what life would've been like for that man had he never been born broken—assuming he'd been born broken—just as he had—after *chronologically* turning into a teen—started to wonder what life would've been like for himself had *he* never been born broken, only to discover *why* before the trial, before that intelligence quotient test was given to him twice—for until then, he had just been told that the reason was a mystery; at night, with his backward boyish mind, he would sometimes see the slow reversal of the torso's time, over and over again, as if on one of those old video cassettes he would always watch while high on hemp, waving his remote to rewind and rerun a certain scene over and over to repeatedly undo something ruthless that'd been done, rewinding so slowly that in the television window on the steel door across the corridor, from under the metal ceiling mesh covering the deeply depressed light fixture, that torso would start swaying and swaying again, only to jerk up a bit, and then the scene would shift in his mind in slow rewind to show the whole human being in his cell— who would be *him* instead of someone else—standing on top of the toilet-sink and unlooping the tightly twisted ligature from the holes of the metal ceiling mesh and then sitting on his bed with his hands now working and working over the long unraveling shreds—occasionally shoving them under his bed to pick up a book before a face would appear before the steel door's window—but then the shreds would come cleanly and wholly together again after meeting his teeth to form a single white sheet—which he would soon snuggle underneath: risen to become recumbent. That dulcet voice from the ventilation vent had told the nephew that the guards had taunted the man, that the mesh was warped from his weight, that a bit of bright purple was bitten off between his teeth. That he had soiled himself. And until the fourth night the voice had sounded so nice, so sweet, for a man's, but then the nephew seemed to have heard just how hollow and tinny it was, as if it were inside an up-side-down strainer, as if it were some venomous honeybee that could still squeeze itself out through a hole, for even the nephew's faulty mind could still find a fault or two in what was being said, night after night. I'm not stupid, he said, on the fourth night, this thing up here can't hold anybody and the holes are too tight and tiny, and the voice said, You're right, but don't you *want* to believe it? If a man really wants to, indeed, he

could even sit down to do it, and then the voice pro-
ceeded to tell him how he could and how he couldn't
stop wondering, the nephew, if *it* were even possible,
couldn't stop wondering not even after two more
nights, after the voice had constructed a rope in his
head, from his own bedsheet—so thoroughly that he
could even *de*construct it in his head—just couldn't
stop wondering, for once the man felt faint and frightened all he would have to do is sit up and untie the
rope—Which you say he *could* squeeze through this
window wire, right?—for his hands would have to be
free to make that—What you call it?—that noose and
to work that—Give it again?—that knot that simple
knot. Yes, would not this man just sit up once he felt
faint and frightened and undo the damn knot? But
the voice was silent now, and the nephew was proud,
for he had thought it through—something he just
couldn't do with those two detectives—as if he had just
taken another test and passed it because it couldn't be
done. But then the voice explained it to him again,
very slowly, like it did with the rope, and said that this
man—while sitting beneath the metal window mesh
with his rope a little slack, his back against the wall—
could just lean to his side any side and simply fall
asleep, from lack of air and blood flow, from the rope
pressing against the vein to the heart and the artery to
the brain—both being on either side of the neck—but
never mind this, for once the man leans over to his
right or to his left—it does not matter—the weight of
his upper body would put him to sleep in less than

twenty seconds, so that if someone were to sing Happy Birthday as he did it, no doubt, he would fall asleep before the first verse was over: For if you *really* wanted to do it, said the voice, all you would have to do is to hold your will. Hold my what? Don't sit up. Your weight would put you to sleep and then your sleep would do the rest—for you would fall asleep in *half* the time it would take me to sing Happy Birthday to you. So that now in the visiting booth, behind the glass, the uncle just found himself staring, mute, until he found himself speaking again: So *this* is who told you to? *Taught* you to? This voice? Get it out of your head, he said, *right* now—because we *can't* bring you back with a fucking remote! But then he looked over the nephew's shoulder, at the guard looking in through the steel door's window, and calmed himself, taking a deep breath. I'm sorry, he said. But the nephew had already put his head down on his desk and didn't say a thing, and stayed like that for a while. Are you still there? the uncle facetiously said, trying to make light, for when his sister visited, with their receivers to their ears, both mother and child would have their heads down on these slim opposing desks, when there was nothing left to say with time still left, nothing left to do but to listen to each other's breath. Are you still there? And while holding his receiver to his ear, with his head still resting on his other hand, the nephew nodded sideways. That voice, said the uncle, very solemnly now, was either an inmate or a guard trying to hurt you. Don't listen to it. Sit up. *Sit* up. You're almost home. But even after he *was* home, day after day, month after month, he ate too much and slept too late—risen to become recumbent—and from time to time he would still hear the red advice from the voice: for in the county jail complex, after trying to *hang up*, he sat up and just sat there, until the guards discovered him. Don't sit up don't sit up, said the voice, from time to time, for his self-preservation instinct still needed to be overridden. Yet, eventually, after that monthlong residency in the county jail complex, after being beaten by the guards for ripping up his sheet—with those two suits concealing the bruises for the ongoing trial—after being home and beaten by white police— for his story was everywhere—after over a year and a half of being a proxy-freed offender and a murderer and a coward—ruthlessly harassed by initiative ministries—after living with the guilt and the grief and quite possibly the grace that could come from freeing his proxy—no one knows for sure what he was hoping for, for he didn't leave a note—unemployed and unemployable at twenty-four, the nephew decided not to sit up anymore, for on a snowy morning in mid-January, after a double shift at the hospital, his mother had come home and heard him in his room while she was scowling at the wrappers and the cartons on the living room coffee table—for the condemned had consumed three cheeseburgers, two large orders of fries, three slices of peach pie, and two slices of pound cake—and she would believe later that night and maybe for the rest of her life that had she just gone into her son's room all aggressive and upset she might've been able to speak to him about something a little bit more serious than untidiness—but she was just too tired to be belligerent, so she retired to her room. That night she found the mess still there. She called for him twice, but there was no answer. She walked down the half-lit hallway to his room and turned the knob and pushed the door, but met stiff resistance, for the door cracked a bit but wouldn't move anymore, as if her son were trying to hide something or someone inside and so she told him to move away, but still there was no answer no light and so she sniffed inside instead, for she had caught him with a whore before, but instead of perfume or a fuck she could only smell the ammonia of someone's rancid piss, so that now so that now she could only think about his syncopal episodes that had started after the police assault and that he could've possibly passed out as he sometimes passes out and the more she thought about it the harder she pushed and the wider the crack became, and only then, by the hallway's half-light, could she see, tied to the inside door knob, the gloss of a slim leather belt. She felt around for and flipped the inside light switch and something in her left her, and then she pushed and pushed against it, the door, as hard as hard as she could until she could squeeze through a bit but the body was still blocking it, being two hundred and fifty-two pounds now and leaning sideways as *she* was leaning sideways and in too awkward a position to undo the belt which was too taut and too tightly tied with only one of her hands available, for she couldn't get her other shoulder through, neither could she pull up the body *by* a shoulder to create enough slack to untie the knot at the same time, and so she just *pulled* the goddamn belt and then *immediately* let it go, stepping back from the door, and began kicking and kicking it until she could get her other shoulder through, yet she was *still* in such an awkward position that she couldn't get the other arm down, so that now, halfway through the door, she just cried. Then her wits returned and she ran into the kitchen and came back and cut the belt, and after pushing some more, she was able to step over the body and into the room. She undid the belt, she opened his eyes, but his face had a bluish ashen tinge to it, his tongue was bloated and protruding considerably, and his sclerae were bespeckled by burst blood capillaries. He never had time to hold his will. For after sitting up with a bottle beside him, with a high level of spirits in his system, his trousers darkened where the pant legs met, he passed out—so that he never even knew that he was dying . . . .

February has come and the cold hurts now. The skies have lost their blue and have cast a grey stillness instead. The windchill factor has been sharpened by a strop, so that now it is very painful for any shopper to venture out. Farmers are weary; the water in their barns turns to ice, the chickens cannot drink it, the goats cannot lick it, and inside their houses, due to a power surge, the chicks' beaks—no longer gaping like the sweet gumball pods in the summer—are all melted shut from the kisses of portable heaters. Pipes freeze and the ancient trucks refuse to turn over, the cold kills the power, and the provincials exchange instructions to navigate each other through. Snow on a decadent city would make the pavement look like a pageant queen, a daylily for a day, yet the piss and the tailpipes would soon exhaust fine wear—while in the retrograde territories of the north, in north country, in the wind and the snow on the iron earth, the cold is an oracle: nature is an engraver, a burin to the bones, scraping and scraping: I want you to die, it inscribes, its says, tonight, and I will make it so easy for you. Everything you own will be returned to me in tatters or decomposing matter, so there is no one you can hold onto that my embrace will not release. So why not give it all back to me immediately? How willing are you to resist? How deeply are you willing to let go, if you wish to relinquish all of this? No secrets no pacts no plastics— they only create a cancer in me. Experience this joy of loss now, this heavenly state of impermanence. Enjoy your death by living it longer, more fully, by understanding it deeply. That is love. For quality has nothing to do with time. Quality is the keenest of perception. And I swear to you you will not be around to understand these things later. But why, a woman asks, for her man and herself, why did we come here? You did not come here, it says, it inscribes. So, the woman says, we cannot lie to ourselves in the snow—yet we need we need to get away from the attrition of this forest, from the cancer of this cabin: the house is haunted. The house is not haunted: you are. The wind buffets the windows. The vagina and the clitoris are the vocal cords now, the mucus membranes vibrating as she sits astride the man. The truth is long and wide and singular, she says, and it is for us—it has always been for us. Grows fuller inside of her. At night, she says, the truth is at war with us. It wants us to die. It wants us to love. For it fights for beauty. And it attacks with our hearts. It attacks with our hearts. The wind buffets the windows. The night passes, and then an aubade is being boasted by a bird brave enough to weather it. A cedar, permanently bent by the wind, is catching a red cardinal in her lee, while in her bed, in the warmth of it, the woman awakens to the man—animated by the sun. His hand is over her breast, as she smells the bad breath of his dream, and soon his tongue is circling over the fine Braille around her nipple; her fingernails sink into his bushel of hair, raw black cotton, shot with shocks of white, as he sucks the phantom milk, as his other hand glides over her warm abdomen and straight jet black patch and into the quick—and soon the woman is dewed. He is holding her other breast now, sucking ferociously, with her thick liquids oozing into the palm of that other hand, his two fingers rubbing the upper ridges of her muscular sex, which feels like the upper ridges of his mouth—so that his mouth is now meeting her nether mouth, with her breath catching and resuming, catching and resuming. She grips the bushel. His tongue is flicking her clitoral glans now as the two fingers are making a motion of *come hither come hither* to that which is lost inside it, the vale, massaging the upper ridges amidst the mounting suspirations, and then firmly pressing upward as the coywolf pressed upward and into the hilly wood—she has an urge to evacuate her bladder, but not her bladder, then inhales as her back arches and flattens with the exhalation: the urge passes as she apexes and forces the fingers out, her palms jutting out, pushing his forehead away, as he swallows the last of her jet. Afterward, slightly spasmodically, she lies, with her legs akimbo and her arms stretched out between her thighs, as if frozen in the thrust, eyes shut. Your skin is a maze, he says, after a while, propped up on an elbow. He is scanning the recumbent nakedness of her nearly hairless body, her arms now relaxed. I see a maze in you. A route. I see a labyrinthine route. It is circuitous and is sinking down into your flesh like a compression mold, my love, your body your whole body is covered by it, your forehead your face—my God, don't you ever go! I love you. And then she presses her chest against his to roll him onto his back, holding his face in her hands as her eyes hold his and says, very tenderly: What are we to pull away with? And then her nails are softly scraping his stomach, combing the black kinky patch to hold him, and soon she mouths him—his dream returns to him: he is fully formed in front of a monstrous tree, a colossus covered with cicadas instead of leaves, thousands upon thousands of cicadas vibrating the tree like a towering tuning fork stabbed into the dirt, as he stands naked and erect, as these tymbals rattle it and the ground around it while sucking the life from him—for as the harsh round sound of these murderous abdomens fill the air, slowly his stomach sucks in, his ribs rise, and his eyes tumefy: My love my love, he says, you are killing me! And so she sits up and fits him in, mounts him so that they can be the same again, the lover and the inverted lover—as though a thermal inversion line must exist where the sexes come together, a Fata Morgana in the Garden, a high card from the Tarot. Come and see, it says: the girl and the boy are the oracle. Hours later though, alarmed, the woman awakens the man. He is sobbing. It is noon and the sky is overcast; the belief is a few feet of snow, the forecast called for it. Fern frost proliferates on the windows, the furnace has long since died down, and the space heater has grown somewhat insufficient. He tells her he had another dream: it is dark and he is seeing her sitting beside him in the projector's light at the local cinema—as they were last week—and they are watching an oldish foreign film concerning three sisters of means in a mansion with a stout modest servant, a younger mother of God, and one of the sisters is dying of uterine cancer on her bed in the servant's lap, a Pietà, a triangle with the head of the servant at the apex and her hands and the head of the mistress below her bare breast forming the base, the film was the first color film for the filmmaker, or the second or the third, and red was the palette, the color inside the dragon, the interior of the soul, and the man tells her that she is munching on a tub of popcorn, very brashly, as if purposefully, and once the film is over they are driving through the snowy nightscape on the snowplowed route when a buck bolts across, and he swerves and succeeds in staying on the road, but she is shocked and snaps at him when he tries to console her, for his tone came across as condescending—and these scenes so far are so similar to the real event a week ago, though *she* was the one who was driving and *he* was the one who had gotten livid—but then the scene shifts and they're in the cabin again being surprised by a party, an intimate party of strangers, he thinks he knows them but knows none of them, so he leaves the party and goes down a small hall and into a room that's not supposed to be there and meets a woman in another room that's not supposed to be there either— or is it?—a dwarfish figure, grandmotherly almost, who generates a boyish compulsion in him, yet when he drops to a knee to hug her, like an old demonic cat, she bites the back of his neck, and he feels a terrible constriction between his shoulders, a shock along the spine, and angered he calls her Cunt, she bites down harder, he collapses, he calls her Cunt again and can catch the crunch of his bones—Cunt! Cunt! Cunt!— until the woman wakes him up: his cries having awakened *her*. He is sobbing. He is pushing against the backside of her now, with her on all fours and with his fingers in the creases of her pelvis. He is hot. He is scared. He is no longer in the Garden. But more hours have passed and the man is gone, so now the woman is sitting in her chair, in the living-dining room, with the snow freshly falling on the cedar outside, forever bent forever bowed, sitting at her weathered wooden desk, attempting another letter to their benefactor, hers and his—the *second* letter that's to be sent express mail—with the man still unware of the first. She has been sitting here for over an hour now: the second letter has yet to be written, just as that first letter had yet to be answered and would *never* be answered in words, only in action—for the *proof* that that letter had been read and answered right now is in town, braving the elements, purchasing groceries and some home supplies and maybe even *waiting* to purchase something as a last-minute decision from her. Marry me, the man said, said it after he did it. But beforehand he had asked if she was sure, if she was certain, for she had asked him to and there was no contraception, but she just held him and didn't say a thing, held him tightly as her quadriceps tautened in a split, with the hallux of each foot pointing in opposite directions—as if she were opened to it at the time and at the same time not, the insemination, the notion being possibly foolish if not downright wrong and doing nothing about it even now—for this recent dream of his is nothing but another version of *hers*, of her recurring dream: his party of strangers is her pack of wolves—her lesser selves, the lowest being the dreamer, her, for he's fretting and dreaming as her—the dwarf is the black wolf—the creator and the destroyer—and the party is the departure. The man has subsumed her into himself. Or is it the other way around? For now she thinks: Was this why I asked him to do it—after I have long told him *not* to do it? Have I absorbed him into myself? Have I decided to stay and is this my way to assure him that I *will* should my mother ever call—as far as he knows—despite already telling him this? She thinks and thinks about this while still not calling him from the landline to their shared cellular phone before the storm, with her last-minute decision to buy some emergency contraceptives: her pills. Marry me, the man said, and she said nothing—for is this *his* way to ensure she would stay should her mother ever call, as far as he knows, despite her already telling him she would? Or is this just his forethought to legitimatize it, the child, should she become gravid? For she hasn't spoken of the first day of spring to him and of the possibility it may bring in accordance with her mother's call—they never speak of her brother anymore—but though the man does not know a thing about the brother's resentencing hearing in March, still, the possibility of his appeal being heard *one* day, of him receiving the same sentence again, has been *eating* at him ever since she first wrote to him—despite her fidelity: the man knows better than anyone that only after a sentencing or a resentencing hearing can a proxy come forth, no other time—provided of course that the sentence is capital on both occasions—and that a person's mind may change over time. It is fortunate that they're in the forest, she thinks. He won't hear of any resentencing hearing up here, from any media, for if he continues to remain secluded as he chooses, for the most part, in north country, it is not difficult to know nothing of the outside world, if only for the winter: the television is nonexistent; her sleek portable computer, her cellular and landlines, her old radio he hardly ever uses. No one at the university or in the town would ever bring up her family to him—let alone any sensitive information pertaining to them—for in fact, other than the Bhikkhunis, no one even *knew* of her family, until after the touring began. No one knows of the disownment. Yes, it is fortunate that they came here, though they have always been here. She wanted their time together to be free of any feelings of uncertainty, but after that mid-December phone call from their benefactor, hers and his, she is now left with the possibility that her promise might have to be kept, and much sooner than later—that promise she made in the first letter—and that she would have to continue to keep it a secret from him until the end of March. Marry me, the man said, said it while still inside of her, growing smaller, and her hand just wiped away the sweat from his forehead—but now, looking out the window at her weathered wooden desk, the woman is feeling the conflict of hope taking hold in her uterus, a great reason to renege, a great reason to write another letter, for on one of the coldest days of the season, sixteen degrees below zero, she is feeling the light and the warmth right now. But then the wind buffets the windows again, reminding her of her promise, of that archaic custom: boys over girls. It is a game of chess and certain pieces must be forfeited. Her mother knows this. For *if this one goes awry,* if this resentencing hearing goes her way, her mother meant, though her son may never be able to rule over the company publicly, given the controversy, his technological genius could still guide it from *behind* a proxy—just as *she* had guided it from behind her husband. The king is the legacy and the strategy—before she dies—is to advance a specific pawn across the board to become another queen. The woman's thoughts now stray again to the route that led her to this road: after she learned of the man's case, from that film that was done on him and on others like him, she learned the rest of it from his sister, who had already been campaigning and soliciting publicity for a year; she helped his sister organize protests and solicit more publicity, as he continued to do what he *could* do from inside, give interviews and write about the plight—for the possible prints and biological evidence on that article of clothing near the crime scene was the key to everything; but after the man was sent to the psychiatric unit last year, last January, after the woman wrote that first letter for fear of his possible suicide (though her mother may have waited *months* after reading it, for the news came in June), once steps were taken, it may have only taken a *week* to do what the protests and the defense couldn't do in *years*—for her mother's affluence and influence had finally procured the microscopic truth: confirmation of the nephew's innocence. With a request or a threat or a furtive monetary inducement presented to an official in the city of the committed offense, with a simple phone call to the district attorney or, most likely, to the mayor himself—given the infamy of the case—the mother was able to have that article of clothing released to the new defense team: this scenario is the most likely, for she has yet to state the contrary. Due to the incompetency and the poor acumen of that court-appointed attorney—who had never tried a capital case—he had never even *asked* to have that article of clothing analyzed, for fear it could've incriminated his client—despite the family's request to have it tested—and was mistaken in his confidence that he could counter the client's confession without it, as well as discredit the testimonies of the witnesses against him, his underage associates. That clumsy court-appointed attorney couldn't even effectively put forth strong mitigating circumstances during the sentencing hearing, despite his client's deprived background and his mental deficiency—due to the gross indiscretions of the parent—for even though this mental deficiency had been wrongfully dismissed before the trial, it *still* needed to be brought up again at the sentencing hearing, to sway the jury instead of the judge, but it wasn't. So that in order to save the proxy from the capital sentence, the new defense team, paid for by private support, had attempted to have that article of clothing analyzed after the proxy received his stay—which could've been taken away at any time—a stay granted two months after the proxy had been imprisoned (either due to the public outcry or to the state's inability to attain the medicines it uses for executions, for domestic and foreign pharmaceutical companies are very fearful of their misuse, so they say). That article of clothing needed to be released by the prosecution, allied not only with the police and the forensic lab but with the city district attorney, and the mayor most likely, due to the infamy of the case, for like that clumsy court-appointed attorney—so incompetent that he seemed to be in cahoots with the circus—the *prosecution* sought to keep that article of clothing from being analyzed, for it didn't want to have to admit it was trying the wrong person, and sacrifice a case that was intended to build careers. The new defense team needed to have that article of clothing released and analyzed by an *outside* agency, but the prosecution—whose former head is now the city district attorney—called the request a *fishing expedition*, especially since the original defendant had confessed to the crime and there were collaborating witnesses; the defense, it claimed, had no good-faith basis for believing that there were any prints or any biological evidence on that article of clothing that would point to someone *other* than the original defendant—and the judge, after months and months, would eventually agree. No, the prosecution didn't need or even *want* to bring up that article of clothing at the trial, for though the glove might have fit the nephew physically, the information in the perspiration would not have fit him genetically, nor would the prints have fit his—for the glove was undeniably involved in the crime; the *victim's* biological evidence was all over it, generously so, after the hammer had entered his head, again and again and again: according to the detectives, as stated on the stand, the perpetrator had obviously noticed the victim's egregiously white skin in a neighborhood full of deprived blacks and his staunch routine of ministering to women in a nearby shelter at night, and on the night of the murder he had found the victim's vehicle parked as usual on a side street behind the shelter and slashed a tire, and then waited in the dark of the adjacent alley, so that when the victim came out and bent down and was inspecting the said tire the perpetrator had come up quickly and quietly from behind and struck the first blow, and then the second and the third and the fourth; yet, though those detectives might've been right about the murder being premeditated, they could've been wrong about the premeditator being a male; the victim's pockets and vehicle were rifled through, for of course his wallet was never found, nor was the green pouch containing the weekly donations from his congregation, which must've been in the vehicle that night, according to the church secretary, who was supposed to have deposited it at the bank that afternoon but couldn't because she was too sick and had to deposit herself in bed instead; the victim must've been planning to do it the next day, because it was never done; the perpetrator left the hammer by the body and raced down the alley and threw the gloves down a storm drain: the hammer was brand new and stolen and had neither any prints nor any biological evidence on it from the perpetrator, but one of the gloves had landed on a ledge under that storm drain, where it was found just after the confession; but as far as the detectives were concerned, it no longer mattered. And now it would've been better if that glove had *never* been found, for to this day, since it reopened the case, the perpetrator has yet to be identified. The woman now turns away from the window, from the falling snow outside, and looks around the cabin, at the life she is living. Of course she hasn't told the man's sister about the first letter either.

No, she has never talked about what she has done or about what she may have to do to a woman she's grown quite close to in their silent sisterhood of very fine grief, both having confided in each other, being bereaved of children, and both believing that they *themselves* were the reasons for their bereavements. Ever since they started collaborating together, these two from two different classes and races, the woman would often come down from the forest into the sister's city or some other city so they could join up with protesters to publicize the case, and once or twice to find a legitimate suspect *other* than the one convicted of the crime—the sister's son, whom the woman had met on several occasions, yet had never gotten to know or to talk to, due to his recently developed reticence—interviewing both the victim's secretary and the victim's daughter, who after the suicide of the sister's son had spoken out on the man's behalf. The woman came down from the forest to the city to succor the sister when she was freshly grieving, to help finalize the funeral, to attend it, and then to stay on for a little while afterward to listen, for on that one night in the sister's apartment, as a consoler and a sounding board, she lovingly listened to the alcohol-induced self-abuse of the sister's rant, to the full damnable resurgence of the sister's sins, which were brought up before the trial by that court-appointed attorney— before that intelligence quotient test was given to her son, in hopes of proving him *ineligible* for capital consideration, if convicted, and which *should've* been brought up at the sentencing hearing as well, but hadn't been—sins which her son was *just* now hearing about and would have to be explained to him by her later, how he had been irreparably born broken by something stupid she had done—more than once—by exposing him to the *needle* in utero; the woman listened to the sister's difficulty in coming to terms with her son's disability, to her long-standing sobriety, to her fixation on her hospital work much later—not merely for the money or for the good will but for the moments away from home—and to her fixation on her brother's fate—which had tragically taken the remainder of her attention away from her newly traumatized son. On that night, at that moment, the woman as a consoler and a sounding board could have given the sister the update that she had just written and sent a short letter for help, to help alleviate some of the grief; yet instead, she just listened and listened and stared up at the ceiling later, trying to sleep, now looking and listening with her eyes to the alcohol-induced self-abuse of the juvenile handwriting on it—while lying on the dead boy's bed. No, she didn't tell the sister about the letter, because the sister would have rightly asked, either verbally or silently: Why didn't you write it before? And then the truth would've shone through the shame—though *surely* the sister would've understood why not, indeed, she would've been intensely *against* it, the proposal. But why did I *really* not write it before? the woman asked herself, lying on the dead boy's bed. Because she just wasn't ready. She just wasn't ready to ask for help from a hateful heart; she just wasn't ready to forfeit her fairy-tale ending, her hopes of a new life, of absolution for the man and for herself—*without* the help from a hateful heart. For this is what the help would entail: a life for a life. Once more. Once again. After she started writing the man, after that first month—when she *knew* she was in the love, the province of love—it would have still been *five* months before the sister's son would suicide, so there would've been *more* than enough time for that short letter to be sent and received and responded to. It took the suicide of the sister's son and the lunacy of the man for her pride and her hope and her fear to disappear—for a while—for that letter to be written, for contact to be made with that hateful heart. It took that letter to be written for her lover's long letters to be burned, to be thrown into the furnace—in a sad attempt to decathect from him: to remain in the now and only the now and never be undone. And once that glove was finally released, naturally, it was readily assumed by everyone other than her that the governor, under public pressure—not the mayor pressured by bribery or threat or favor—had finally relented: November elections were approaching and the governor—who wished to remain in the good graces of his constituency—could still save face somehow. And he did. The woman gasps, sitting at her weathered wooden desk. Yes, she says, as the consoler and the sounding board to herself. Yes, she thinks, as the wishful thinker—for the first time, having thought she knew the truth—this *is* what could have happened.

Couldn't it? So that maybe my mother didn't do anything at all? For she never wrote back nor said anything over the phone about having done something—I've just been *assuming* she did—and if she said she *had* done something, maybe it would've just been a lie? Maybe she's just playing on this serendipitous turn of events? Maybe she's just playing on a promise? For all this seems so insidious to me. It reminds me of trapping and fur trappers, of the perpetrators and their victims, the detectives and their suspects, the mothers and their daughters: trappers tend to be loners, and trapping tends to involve hard hiking through unpleasant territories and daily dedication to the tending of the traplines; and then there is the unpleasant part of skinning and cleaning the pelts, and finding the best uses for the carcasses, but in essence it is quite simple: find where the animals are hunting and feeding, set a line of steel kill traps with the bait, return in a day or two, remove the dead and reset the traps. Carcasses are often the very bait. Or the meat is ground up for dog food or seasoned for sausage. Or the remains are simply burned or buried: all those proliferating nuisances dispatched by permission of annual permits. But *slotha*, she thinks, sitting at her weathered wooden desk, slotha is a form of trapping too. Prayer, like listening, is setting a trap for God . . . .

Mother, my warrant will be signed. But you can save me. You can save me from myself. For though I cannot imagine you will save me, your daughter, I still must imagine it. For the injection chamber, I imagine, like some disaster sites, will smell of sex in spite of the forest-scented disinfectants. An attorney told me this once, at a bar; she was very distraught: on the face of her legal adversary, that very day, she had witnessed the news of a posthumous acquittal for a man who had been put down for a house that had been burned down, bony bodies in the rubble; but when she was first investigating the scene she had smelled the faint scent of sex—and it would be this same scent outside the injection chamber on the other side of that glass, suffusing the witness room: You should imagine your death, the man had said, there is nothing more beautiful, said this while strapped down to a table that had been partly angled upward by a button, forty-five degrees at the waist, as if he were lying in an adjustable hospital bed, talking to visitors, said this not

to the families of the victims or to the deputy director or the
director of the prisons, but to this prosecutor in the bar with
me, reciting his last words of sobriety through her joyless in-
ebriety, this condemned woman confiding her compunction to
a could-be condemned woman unaware for when a warrant
is signed a set comes to your cell, Mother, a counselor or a
chaplain is chosen, and then the warden comes with his guards
to ask you to please stand for a formal reading, you are given
a new change of clothes, you go from orange to yellow and too
soon to white as some maturing insect—from affliction to fear
to shock—white when you are to be transformed into the final
flying thing—for your status must always be known—there
is the fear of filling out forms, of where oh where to ship your
belongings and body when the greatest common grave of
man is his mind and you'll be disremembered anyway? or
perhaps ashes sent with pieces of teeth to an attorney? most
proxies are women, for most women are proxies for men, my
lover having been the exception—for they once measured
him for a moment for a suit, the guards, said either partici-
pate or be beaten, and I might've even said to them or to one
of them as he said, for my lover and I are one, that you can
get into my head, sir, but that would mean you are out of
yours, and then they would beat us anyway, beat us then
and before then, beat us at the behest of their boss, the
warden, who had had our ankles bound and our wrists
shackled to a waist belt and then brought before him to his
big beautiful office, at night, after everyone else left the
building, as if he were Lucifer himself showing Jesus the
sights from a summit, with a fiery arm around him, prom-
ising him some temporary amenity if he would only believe

in this duality—for the Devil is the belief in duality—but then he had them beat us—for my lover and I are one— right in front of him for doing a series of interviews—for there is this curtain of secrecy inside and we had so rudely drawn it back a little—we were being brutalized while being brutally conflicted for after being and only being in another building for so awfully long, after the fresh air we felt on our face, after that short van ride to the warden's building and seeing the vastness of the parking lot and the sky—indeed the sky, the stars, with no damn chain-link ceiling between us, as it is over our communal stall outside for our one hour a day, six days a week—after seeing the glorious cleanliness of the administrative halls and the vending machines and the plants and the elevator and the big beautiful office, we were now being beaten upon a carpet, something you would only see in a cinema so outrageous and surreal and simply for a few little interviews, to publicize our plight, which had brought bad publicity to the prison, and then after being beaten we were sent to solitary for our ribs and wounds to heal and seal in shadow and gown and sheet, only to be returned to our cell thirty days later with much of our belongings liberated, lifted, confiscated, our headphoned radio, our literary leisure, our magazines, our journals, our lover's long letters—so that we would remain in the now and only the now and never be undone . . . . Yet now you *and* I *are one, Mother, your daughter and you. Our conscience makes it so. Just as you and your son will be one. But I am the lesser of your evils and being the head of an empire you must use the greater evil for the greater good, for the sake of the family legacy.*

*And since our warrant is signed now, yours and mine,
Mother—no more delays from the backlog or from the un-
availability of medicines, or even from that ethical contest
over the initiative itself—since there will be no years or
decades of waiting for an appeal to impede it, our having
waived the right, time has slowly brought us here within
a year. But now time accelerates once your warrant is
signed; if there is no reprieve from the governor, not even
at the last minute, our sentence must be and will be administered. Since the backlog has been eliminated, since the
medicines have been attained from an unnamed source
under the new secrecy statute, since the ethical contest over
the initiative is at a standstill, still, decidedly moot, we will
soon be given a last change of clothes, having gone from
orange to yellow, soon we will go from yellow to white,
from fear to shock, we will be placed inside another cell
under a suicide watch, a week out from administration:
this ruinous intravenous feeding, this low-tech lynching,
will transform medicalized murder into a form of therapy;
it will pervert the instruments of healing and mask the
most despicable act a society can ever inflict upon its citizen
with an antiseptic veneer—and since there are no actual
pharmaceuticals specifically designed for human euthana-
sia, every time this intravenous feeding is used, it is truly
a fatal experiment: the use of well-known pharmaceuticals and medical equipment will blur the line between
patient and prisoner, healing and killing, illness and
sickness, therapy and punishment—which makes the administration all the more menacing. But now we are
clothed in white, Mother, a week out from this, as we sit in*

this ten-foot-high cell that is partially glassed in, the bathroom facilities included; two opposite walls are concrete, while the other two are fashioned from five-foot-high unbreakable glass, with only two and a half feet of concrete coming down from the ceiling and up from the floor—as if the cell itself is the injection chamber, the bed the injection table, as if one glass panel were the one-way mirror concealing the administrator from the spectators, who are all sitting behind that other opposing panel. Everyone is always watching us. We are not to be alone. We are unable to masturbate or to go to the bathroom. Our hair is too long, so we ask for our head to be shaved and in the mirror, with our back straight and our breasts scarcely defined, our frame lean and truculent, our eyelids pulled narrow at the corners by crow's-feet, the bones of our pyra-midal cheeks, the square jaw and the jet-black buzz cut peppered with salt—like a Buddhist nun's—we look quite handsome. Our possessions have all been bequeathed to our soon-to-be survivors, and only our writing implements remain, a spiritual book. Visitors have been given greater access to us. A phone is in our cell. The guards are so nice . . . . On the day of administration, severely anxious, a guard comes to wake us at dawn, but we are already awake—night is the best counsel. We are finally to be transformed at noonday today. The clement call has not come, the pardon, yet the governor still has until the last minute. We have already acquiesced though. We are ready. We are allowed a last meal and shower and this, too, is glassed in, but when the eyes are closed and the mind is open this water cascades from a cliff, from a hot spring, as our skin glistens in the sun and we are clean and given a second chance for a final meal—having refused the first offer—anything we want from a nearby truck stop; we ask for tea and no sugar: we don't have the stomach for anything that won't come out the other end; everyone else though, all the prisoners on the row and off, will have fried chicken for lunch: a tradition since the launch of the electric chair, for over a hundred years. We are to be transferred to the other building now, the final building, and a female orderly is present when they enter this semi-glass cell, giant muscular men in military gear, an intimidation tactic; they shackle us tight, our ankles and wrists cuffed and tethered to a waist belt, and in addition to our orange winter coat we are given a ski cap and some mittens, though our thermals are very thin; the walk is only from the execution unit to the death house next door, but it is arctic out, below zero—yet it is still the freshest and freest air we have breathed ever since we arrived here, early last spring: fresh snowflakes are falling, tiny descending skeletons of snow accumulate on a phalanx outside, many more men in military gear with machine guns here to make sure we are laid to rest without rescue, while beyond the gates are likely a line of news vans and vanguards and a vigil of abolitionists, barricaded in clothes, bundled like beggars for life or sitting inside their vehicles. The death house is freezing. It is only used for this purpose—yet someone should've had the forethought to heat it. They let us keep our winterwear until it's warm inside the cell, next to the injection chamber, a cell which is five-feet wide and eight-feet long; we spend our last three hours here, talking to our advisor, our Buddhist mother nun, who has long since begun to love us like a daughter—we would weep over our prayer beads, if we were allowed any. No phone calls. No visits today. Our visitors have all been heard and seen outside that semi-glass cell yesterday. It is warm now. Our advisor is asked to step out for a moment, so we can undress, so that our arms and our legs and our groin can be shaved, for swift venous access—yet this is nothing new to a woman or to anyone who has so readily acquiesced: we could be on a gynecological visit for all we care, with this female orderly in here, if it weren't for those guards outside; the strap-down team awaits. Eventually we dress again, minus the winterwear, so that our advisor can reenter. The administration has been rehearsed, and though this calculated protocol is always experimental in nature, it is still perceived to be a skillful praxis of painlessness. The administrator, medically untrained, has been drilled to administer the medicines through a set of mechanical syringes fitted by a qualified medic, or a doctor—despite the Hippocratic oath—who will also enter the chamber after the first shot to make a consciousness check and then leave and later return with another qualified medic or doctor, after the third shot, to confirm the cessation of all vital functions. There are, in fact, two administrators, as well as two sets of syringes; several intravenous lines travel from within the administrative room through a hole in the wall to a stand inside the chamber, where they await attachment to two separate needles, which are then fed into two swollen veins, respectively produced by a single tourniquet: one needle is a backup, one person is an impostor, but both are posing *as the impostor because neither wants to be the administrator, for as in the past, when only* one *of the two switches jolted the electric chair, it is essentially the same: one person has a set of dummy drugs, leading into a dummy bag, while the other has the set of genuine drugs—and neither knows who is holding the switch; they can both say that they didn't do it, or they can both regret that they did, for three hundred dollars in cash, for a procedure that should only take ten minutes—but could last for two hours . . . . It is time. We must go on alone. Our Buddhist mother nun says to us: Look on him. He will be sending the love. As will I. And then she kisses our tears, each side of our face, before leaving our cell. Hers is the last loving touch we will ever know, for now we are feeling a room full of people who are afraid to touch us. Yet have to. So that now with small, restricted steps and chains and a military mission of four, between giant muscular men, we walk next door. The doorway to the chamber has an ovality to it, and aside from the vents and the hole in the wall the chamber is an airtight tank made of metal, a gas chamber that was built after the electric chair so that when we step through and over the bottom rim of this final awful egg we begin to feel faint and fall toward the guard who stepped in front of us as another one steps in after us, both holding us up, with the other two remaining outside; the director of the state prisons is here; he speaks to us softly, for already we are coming around, telling us to breathe, to just breathe, the air is coming in through the vents. His voice sounds so hollow. It is a small chamber, only four people can fit, and everything is equally aqua and ugly—as if we are in some* sort of submersible, Mother, feeling the merciless sting of our mercy. Our heart is drumming against the breastbone. Our throat is dry. Our acquiescence has left us. Breathe deeply, the director says, here, lie down. We ask for a sip of water. Lie down first, he says, very warmly, and we do. The table is like an operating table with extended armrests and black straps and three sectional cushions: the outline of a body with its arms splayed out, and with their noticeable holes; the tank is octagonal, so that the table is facing a three-paned window that must look into the witness room, for those semi-circular curtains are closed, and above the table is the one-way mirror; both windows are un-breakable. The strap-down team are three of the four guards, so the director has to step out of the chamber so that the third guard can come in; the fourth stays outside with him. Lie down, says a guard—or does he? We say we already have, and then he tells us to relax, to just relax, and then gives a questioning look to one of the other two— who just looks at him very dimly, as if to calmly remind him that we might be out of our wits. We are the only woman in here, for that female orderly is gone. The men are all white and muscular and each of them has a part of their skinny little yellow woman to strap down now; they uncuff our wrists and ankles, slide away the waist belt, and the chains clunk and resound against the tank floor only so that our wrists and ankles can be bound once more, our shoulders and legs, our forehead. Two of the guards leave, one stays, the one who spoke to us; the doctor or the medic comes in, tells us to relax and inserts the needles, very clinically cold—and we are rolling along only because none of our veins were rolling; yet if they were, rolling in the arms, there is always the back of the hands and the top of the feet, the legs and the groin. Since our head is strapped into place, since we cannot see much but the ceiling and the upper part of the walls, we figure that these intravenous lines have been threaded through the holes in the armrests, but it was the use of those alcohol swabs—prior to the insertion of the needles, now taped below the hollows of our elbows—that was really ironic: perhaps those swabs were hedges against the possibility of a last-minute pardon— for after all this, we should not have to suffer the silliness of an infection. Now the doctor or the medic and the guard leave together. Only we and the director are left. There is a clock in here that doesn't even tick. We ask for that sip, and a guard brings us a cold cup of water with a small flexi-straw, bent at an acute angle—for we are horizontal still—holds it for us for several seconds, and then leaves the cup on the stand before sealing the door behind him; air is coming in through the vents. Breathe deeply, the director says, his voice sounding so hollow—for he is feeling claustrophobic; we can see it on his face. He looks at the clock. He looks at the clock. It smells of nothing in here. Seven minutes have passed. There is a ringing and its ripple—and only now are we aware that there's a phone in here: Yes, the director says, listens, and then yeses again. The governor has spoken. And these yeses must've sounded so tinny on the other end to him. The director hangs up and then picks up the phone again to push a button, looking into the one-way mirror: We've been given a go. Wait for my signal. And his voice must sound so tinny on the other end to them. The microphone is turned on. The table is angled upward at the waist, at forty-five degrees, so that we can now see—you and I—the curtains electronically opening . . . . Our lover's face is the first face we see—we see him almost instantly—a shining serpent is in his face, his face a weeping stone! Our Buddhist mother nun is sitting beside him, calmly weeping as well. Two rows of chairs are arranged in a double semi-circle since the tank is octagonal, with our beloveds in the front row and to the left of us. The lover is so radiant! He is so open that the love just pours all over us! He is a water main—massive in diameter—reaching down from the snowcap of a great glorious mountain, feeding us here in the vale, in the shadow of the valley of the forest, where we are oh so grateful and glad and only realizing now—you and I—that this has all been written before, that we've been put to sleep before, a few times before, even shot heroin once after the death of our son so that now so that now we would rather be anesthetized and paralyzed and then neutralized by potassium chloride, or some cousin to it, than be murdered by any other means. Inside the witness room our two beloveds and the entire rear row, the family attorney, the three journalists, and the three volunteer witnesses, are all looking toward the other five viewers in the front—as these five faces show their wretchedness to me! For you are no longer with me, Mother. For these five faces are not the five faces of the family of the victim— none of them are here—they are the five faces of my family. The family of the victim are not permitted to attend, for this event could be too difficult for them; besides, despite their despair, they have already made their grueling contribution to this belief, to the feasibility of holy reform, by allowing this in the Lamb's name, so that now so that now it is time for the family of the offender and the offender himself *to somewhat reciprocate—for this may be the first edifying phase, for he most certainly must witness this, for if he did not attend, eventually, this sentence would be administered to him, as well, for he is still on parole until all of this is over. So you are holding his hand now, Mother, sitting beside your son, who is right in front of me in the front row, sweating. It is the first time I have seen your faces since the substitution last spring, early last spring, and now your hair is fully white. His almost is. He is shrinking to your size, small and mortified, and his eyes are holding your fears; his back is rigid in his chair—but he is shaking so* horribly *that he is like a pole weakly anchored in a whirlwind. He wants to look away, but knows he cannot; he would be sentenced to several years for it; the deputy director stands by the door to make sure, with two of those muscular guards to either side of him, and there is video surveillance. He hasn't slept in a while, your son, his eyes red and swollen, but he's afraid to close them— the nightmare is real. Do you remember, Mother, do you remember what you said to me at my son's funeral, at that gravesite without a body in it, beside my father's? When a parent dies, you said, the past is gone. But when a child dies, the future is. And then, over a year later, you had another reason to wonder if this family is cursed, and I am looking at you closely now, not critically, for I am feeling compassion for your confusion: I have finally found you a body for that site. The three journalists are now flitting their eyes from me to you repeatedly, feverishly jotting down their impressions on their pads, as if they are sensing the truth from us; but everyone knows that I freely offered myself for this, for the sake of this viable reform, so that now I am looking at a long-forgotten aunt, separating my brother from my lover by sitting between the two—as if she now knows what you have always known but never said anything about, never even acknowledged: the ruin of my youth; and there are two more long-forgotten relatives, sitting on the other side of you. The three volunteer witnesses, the three upstanding citizens most likely solicited and rounded up from the Rotary Club by the director himself, are all sitting stoically, each face a blank space the journalists will fill in later as they deem fit—but the face of the attorney is so sorrowful that it won't need any vivid embellishment: he could* not *have imagined this. Seven witnesses in the front row and seven witnesses in the rear. If this were a traditional execution, if the faces of my family were the faces of the family of the victim, there would be a buffet awaiting everyone afterward—including the prosecution and the execution teams—it is part of the budget. A cooler would sit in a corner, for executions only, and the entire atmosphere would seem like a small social gathering, a picnic indoors, with that low-tech-lynched body still warm and down the corridor. Yet when the state kills it is forced to write* homicide *on the official forms, in the space after* cause of death, *for the word* execution *is ambiguous, merely meaning the carrying out of an executive order.* Homicide *tells the truth. Even if the word* legal *precedes it. A hand touches me. Very lightly. As if it's afraid to touch me. Inside the witness room, standing at the door with the guards, the deputy director adopts an alert look—his eyes are on me—and only now do I respond with a look toward the director of the state prisons, who has just touched me, who has been calling my name, using the honorific title for addressing a single woman—for he's been speaking all along and I've been vaguely aware, taking everything in, for he's since finished greeting and informing everyone in attendance that my brother has been sentenced to die, by proxy, for the murder of a woman whom I've never met, and he would now like to give me a moment to make a final statement. He calls my name again, asking if I heard him, and I ask for another sip. He brings me the cup, and then the water brightens my belly. I look toward the lover. I look toward the lover. He is weeping. He is radiant! Hold me open, I say. Hold me open, my love. And my voice must sound so tinny on the other end to him. The director of the state prisons then, in a quivering voice, says that the governor has given him the sanction to proceed, and with that he turns toward the mirror, raises a hand, and then lowers it . . . . The administration is a three-drug procedure. A strong anesthetic is administered first, pentobarbital, which is utilized to euthanize animals. A flush of saline solution follows to hasten the flow—for flushes will follow all of the shots— but my heart rate has already dropped; I have fallen almost instantly. The doctor or the medic comes in wearing a surgical mask and a head scarf to conceal himself and shakes and shakes my shoulder, calling for me twice, using the honorific title for addressing a single woman—though*

135

I am a married woman without my lover's surname or without my wedding ring, for it was forfeited last evening. The doctor or the medic pronounces me unresponsive and exits the chamber, sealing the door; the consciousness check is complete. The second chemical is administered, the paralytic, the vecuronium bromide which surgeons use to paralyze the muscles of a patient, giving them the appearance of peace, a mask of tranquility—but it is given to me in such a high dose that it stops the lungs and diaphragm. But not the heart. Had that notorious sedative been used instead of the pentobarbital, that midazolam—which the state had used on seven men in seven days last year, the expiration date of the drug itself having set the dates for the seven executions—then perhaps I would be feeling a horrible sensation right now, an inferno of flame and of drowning in my own fluid, for that midazolam would've been ineffective in blocking the effects of the vecuronium bromide—and perhaps my pain would be witnessed now as gasping and choking and flinching, amidst the rise and fall of my stomach. But since now I am completely *paralyzed, no one would know that this cruel and unusual punishment could be happening to me anyway, even* with *the pentobarbital; my body is unable to show even the slightest* possibility *of a drowning and burning sensation, no histrionics here, for this mask could be concealing a nightmare. No one can tell. My hell could be subjective. And as it once was when I was a girl, after a night hag sat on my chest, I could be helpless and horrified right now, still sensate, watching the door to my dark room open to admit a dark figure, who soon looms over the foot of my*

bed with an upraised axe—and as this potassium chloride
is injected into the dreamer, to halt the heart, this greater
burn could be that axe hitting home. The director coughs.
The door is unsealed. The doctor or the medic comes in,
checks the eyes, checks the heart, and then another doctor or
medic comes in to confirm, using the same stethoscope. I am
pronounced dead. The time is recorded. The microphone is
turned off. The curtains are closed . . . .

M arch, the first day of spring, on an obliga-
tory trek through the snowbound vale of
the forest, the Black and Asian couple, as
the provincials have come to know them, are surviving
each other in the wild. The temperature has surely
risen, but the pulse hasn't quickened. The cold sun is no
longer brutal, but bothersome. The days have longer
limbs now, but across the sky brave birds are braiding
patterns with birds of prey. Hope is blooming conflict
and soon the sugar water won't run. Yet, though the
snow is less and fleecy, it is not so useless that the youth
won't still lie in it to make angels from the malaise, to
play as when it was thick and fun to work with, making
fortresses from misfortune. The woodpiles are precari-
ously low, but the livers have higher hopes than the
savers who are holding their breaths: We can live off
of leftovers, as long as we don't have to live in the
shadows. We can live in the shadows, as long as we

don't have to live in the dark. Rowing while stacking the last of their wood. As the sound of each piece as it hits the pile shouts—before the end you will kill me! All from a bruising or an abrasion of sorts, from something that has been accumulating all winter, as though starting with the slight callousness of the dry hands from the grabbing of the wood from the woodpile to shove and shove into the black ashy maw of the fat metal beast, causing an inconsideration at first, a burn, to now grow into these rows, and maybe only to end with a conflagration—with these pieces of bark and soot from the woodstove playing as a precursor, the small burns in the memory cells and in the planks of the wood floor from the flying errant sparks. The lovers are leftovers from everyone else and are sleeping in separate beds, wounded by their godlike ankles, after brooding beside many maples without cognizance of their sap, their nectar; though the provincials see that the maples are still making good on their gold from the great differential of subzero nights and above-freezing days, for weeks and weeks and are regularly being tapped for their sweet woody water, with vessels fixed to spiles in their sunny sides for straight drinking or sugaring, to be boiled outdoors over a fire in a vat, supported by a rocket stove of bricks, forty gallons of sap for one gallon of syrup and its myriad recipes—from maple fudge to maple mousse—or to be completely cooked and crystalized into sugar for that indefinite shelf life. But the lovers, the woman and the man, have been fighting more often over fictional things—prisoners of the imagination—for in late February, four weeks ago, after the woman had witnessed the red-tailed hawk eating the black squirrel's heart, the blood moon in the commode and the centrifugal flood of the flush, the next day, she decisively left her sanitary napkin in the wastebasket, in the man's bathroom: biological evidence—despite his multiple coming-ins without any barrier between them—of his possible impotency, and of her perfect pregnability. Now, strong winds from north of the river stacking new snow onto the old still around and covering the ground against the banks have the lovers retracing their steps, for without them, being so deeply within it, the vale, it would be difficult to navigate the return. They ascend as the sun descends and soon the incline gives way to the snowy sward behind the cabin; a crow caws: its knowledge of the beneficent faces. They enter the antechamber of the cabin when the cabin permits a call, for the north wind, the Bear, has been ruthlessly interrupting the landline until now—though the call *has* been coming through the left-behind cellular, which would've been useless in the vale. The man enters the cold kitchen first—though he doesn't feel the cold yet, due to the good blood circulation from the trek—but it is the woman who brushes past him and answers the call and he is thinking nothing of it, for he returns to the antechamber to shed his winterwear, and then he proceeds unshod downstairs to feed the furnace with the last of their wood. Afterward he retires to his room, closing the door, satisfied to be alone and away from the sweet reach of her questioning claw, her smell of blood, and even if he cared to he would not be able to decipher the few foreign words that are now being sieved through the timber of this low-ceilinged room—this white blood cell, this continuously having the same walls the same bars the same books, nothing changes: you have day and you have night, you have day and you have night—he can only feel the attitude in the vibration of her pacing, her feet still shod in boots upon his freshly cleaned floorboards. Soon he will need to start supper, for they are still eating together and making sure that the other is still eating. They are no longer drinking, though they have not gone so far as to forgo the venom of criticism while the pepper is being passed—for even a common courtesy cannot resist the temptation to be right—and a great truth was once told with a temper, which made it much more deleterious than the lie that might've revealed it. But for now he lies on his bed and contemplates: can he stay here? can he continue? can he survive the spring of her survival tactics? But projecting, he thinks, is believing that someone else is suffering from your failures, from your perceived defeats, and when both parties are projecting, it is like two opposing mirrors: the belief is endless. But belief has no place where the truth is concerned, for if we could just not *want* anymore, he thinks, then we would not fall prey to not having. But even wanting to not want is still wanting. But then he thinks of the bodhisattva, of one who has deferred nirvana for the sake of saving others, of the apophatic prophet, of one who has acquired a knowledge of God through negation, a non-conceptual knowledge, attaining it through the abandonment of trite commercial concepts, as the sculptor would deduct stone to reveal the hidden image—not this not that not this. Or maybe the basic human mind is like space: you cannot hammer a nail into space, you cannot spit on the sky, you cannot soil or sully it. No. Not this not that not this. The human mind is like nothing at all: the absolute end of everything, the diametric opposite of all. It is categorically indescribable. It is not an anesthetic state. It is not a quiet place. It cannot be entered: *Last week I had a dream that the unit was filling up with water, that there was a great flood and we were all still locked in our cells and waiting to be drowned, for all the guards had evacuated the unit except for this one who was still running around and trying to free all one hundred and twenty of us with his one key, for the keys to the control cages had been taken, and while the water rose over the heads of the men on row one who were all asleep and couldn't be saved who couldn't be saved he ran up to row two and turned into a cockroach, and then half the men were trying to step on him while the rest remained asleep, and as the water rose higher and higher I could hear the cries of the men on row three, who were all awake, and could see the cockroach swimming in the water over my head. And in that moment, that breath, I was flooded with so much affection for it, so much love, that I saw how precious all life is.*

And I wanted the cockroach to make it. I wanted the cockroach to make it. But now he is hearing her footsteps coming down the stairs so slowly and decisively that he fortifies himself, securing the door to that most sensitive spot beneath his sternum, ready to deny her entrance upon the slow decisive knock, for she, despite the discord, still considers this as his and her place. But the heart can be opened by words, by tone, if they are carefully aligned like the precise sequence of symbols on a combination lock, so when he hears the soft fragrance of her voice, hesitant, almost diffident, he is *untempted* to deny her and is *shocked* when he sees her face: scarcely can he see the shining serpent in the trace—with the setting sun shooting through the window—that physical change in the brain—that blaze of juvenescence! He rises from his bed, dumb, but bliss is in her lips, the kiss, for when they slowly separate in the light of the sunset her skin is so silent that, like a ladybug fixed on a skim of milk, a word from him would barely break through: for a full life, it is said, may be one ending in such an affinity with the non-self—with no one—that there is no self to die.

ENDNOTES

p. 10: *There is no discernible difference between killing a child and killing a sleeping man.* Fernando Pessoa, *The Book of Disquiet* (New York: Penguin Group, 2002).

p. 24: *Suicides have a special language . . . . Like carpenters, they want to know which tools. They never ask why build.* Anne Sexton, *Collected Poems: Wanting to Die* (New York: Houghton Mifflin, 1981).

p. 88: *Capital punishment is the most premeditated of murders . . . .* Albert Camus, "Reflections on the Guillotine," *Resistance, Rebellion, and Death* (New York: Alfred Knopf, 1960).

p. 121: *Slotha* is the Aramaic word for prayer: "to set a trap."

ACKNOWLEDGMENTS

Much gratitude to Mumia Abu-Jamal, a world crusader, who, though no longer on death row, is still prejudicially imprisoned today; and to Kalief Browder, for standing tall for as long as he did. Gratitude to Amy Donnella, a death row attorney of over three decades, who sat with me for over twenty-five hours, over dinners, over phone calls, helping me to understand a little of what has happened, and is still happening, to the condemned in this country; and to her colleague, Eric Motylinski, who shared with me his experience of witnessing an execution. Gratitude to Michael Mejia, a gentleman of words, who gave me the peace of mind of his line edits— by mostly knowing what *not* to edit. Gratitude to the Defender Association of Philadelphia and the Southern Center for Human Rights for their unwavering work— though they both could still use so much support—and to PEN America, the University of Pennsylvania, the University of Alabama Press, and Fiction Collective Two for helping this book come to fruition.